Royal Quest

BOOKS BY RACHEL BRANTON

Lily's House Series
House Without Lies
Tell Me No Lies
Hearts Never Lie
Your Eyes Don't Lie
Broken Lies
No Secrets or Lies
Cowboys Can't Lie

Finding Home Series
Take Me Home
All That I Love
Then I Found You

Other
How Far

Town Called Forgotten
Kiss at Midnight
This Feeling for You
Reason to Breathe

Royals of Beaumont
Royal Kiss
Royal Quest
Royal Dance
Royal Time

Picture Books
I Don't Want To Eat
Bugs
I Don't Want to Have
Hot Toes

UNDER THE NAME TEYLA BRANTON

Unbounded Series
The Change
The Cure
Protectors
Ava's Revenge
Mortal Brother
Set Ablaze
The Escape
The Reckoning
Lethal Engagement
The Takeover
The Avowed

Other
Times Nine

Imprints Series
First Touch (prequel)
Touch of Rain
On The Hunt
Upstaged
Under Fire
Blinded
Street Smart
Hidden Intent
Checked In

Colony Six Series
Insight (prequel)
Sketches
Visions
Travels

Royal Quest

RACHEL BRANTON

WHITE
STAR
PRESS

This is a work of fiction, and the views expressed herein are the sole responsibility of the author. Likewise, certain characters, places, and incidents are the product of the author's imagination, and any resemblance to actual persons, living or dead, or actual events or locales, is entirely coincidental.

Royal Quest (Royals of Beaumont Book 2)

Published by White Star Press

Printed in the United States of America
ISBN: 978-1-948982-29-0
Year of first printing: 2022
Yeas of first electronic publication 2017

Fairy tales in the kingdom of
Beaumont are real...

Amelia

"Excuse me, miss. I need more towels." The voice came from close—far too close.

I dragged my stare from my phone and let it wander up from the man's sandaled feet and tan plaid swimming suit to his bare chest, which I was surprised to find only six inches away from my nose. A very wide, strong chest, with well-defined muscles that made me want to reach out and touch them.

Taking a quick leap back, I pulled my gaze higher to his golden eyes, which were what most women would call yummy. I wouldn't. No, I knew what yummy guys wanted, and in the two weeks I'd been in Beaumont, I'd been hit on by more rich brats than in all my college career at Stanford.

"You do speak English, right?" he asked with a British accent, which wasn't unusual because most Beaumontians I'd met had learned English from British teachers. His hair was brown, but a color light enough to be uncommon in Beaumont. "I asked you several times for towels in French, but you didn't respond."

"You think I work here?" I should have bitten my tongue before I spoke, but the words were already out. I guess the part of me that kept wanting to touch his chest also wanted him to know that I had graduated at the top of my class and had a real job waiting for me back in the States.

See? All yummy did was ruin a girl's plans. What did I care if he looked as sexy as the actor Chris Hemsworth?

One of his eyebrows rose in a very lazy—and attractive—arch. Okay, way better than Hemsworth. "You're wearing one of their uniforms," he said. Then, as if an afterthought, he added, "And it's exactly the color of your eyes." His own golden eyes caressed my face, which was probably turning a bright shade of red. Slowly they wound their way down to my lips.

I did *not* move toward him. I swear. But how did we get so close—again?

Okay, so I *was* wearing one of the ridiculously bright blue maid uniforms, but I wasn't wearing a name tag, my blond hair was down and spilling everywhere, and I had my multi-colored bag over my shoulder. Anyone with brains could see I was off duty. He obviously had more brawn than brains, and even if it was decidedly delicious brawn, I was not impressed in the slightest.

"So unless you just collect uniforms . . ." His smile felt as if someone had turned on the sun. He was maybe a little breathtaking.

And a distraction I couldn't afford. I'd come to Beaumont for one purpose only. After that, it was back to Washington where my real job—my real life—was waiting. "The towels are in baskets by the pool," I told him.

"There aren't any in the baskets. My friends and I looked."

I barely stopped myself from stomping my foot and throwing

my bag at him in frustration. Probably because it was three in the afternoon, and I'd been working since four a.m. I'd had only a half hour lunch break, right before I unclogged three toilets, cleaned up vomit in the lounge, and spent a frustrating hour explaining to an American woman why she couldn't stay in the royal suite—all while her teenage son kept trying to kiss me so he could post our picture on Facebook.

At the moment, I didn't care about the lodge, my reason for coming to Beaumont, or anything else. I'd only been here two weeks, and I'd already had more than my fill of this so-called picturesque little country nestled near the French border between Switzerland and Germany. No matter what the media said, it wasn't all it was cracked up to be.

Maybe my attitude had something to do with it, but at least I was realistic where fairy tales were concerned. They didn't happen, not to girls like me. I didn't even *want* a fairy tale. Fairy tales didn't tell the truth about what happened after. They didn't talk about the infidelity, venereal disease, or car accidents that took people away before you had a chance to really know them.

"Then we're out of towels," I told him. "Completely out. It's all the tourists, you know. Sorry."

"Oh, I see." He didn't move and neither did I, trapped by those beautiful eyes. My knees felt wobbly, and I wanted to reach out and grab something, but there was only him and his glorious chest. Maybe with that hair, he wasn't a Beaumontian at all. He could just as well be one of the many tourists that bombarded the country after the prince—now king—married an American girl.

"I'm Damien," he said, and his voice sent a tingle down my back and over my arms, as if he'd touched me. "What's your name?"

My heart thumped erratically inside my chest. Why did this gorgeous man want to know my name? I wanted to tell him. I also wanted to lean in a bit further and let his lips brush mine. Or at least give him my phone number.

No! I stopped myself before I moved another inch. That would be a mistake. I wouldn't be here long enough for a romance, and I wasn't into casual relationships. Never again.

The door leading to the indoor pool banged and another male voice began speaking in rapid, German-flavored French, the native language of Beaumont. Since I'd studied French all of three months, I understood only the gist of what he said, but my imagination filled in the rest: "So where are the towels? Service has hit bottom with all these stupid tourists invading us." And, "Oh, baby, who's the hot chick?"

The new man was a typical Beaumontian, with dark hair and eyes. A mocking twist marred his full lips, and his demeanor screamed wealth and pampering. He was positively the type to get a woman fired for not getting him towels.

"She's American." Damien's gaze seemed to delve inside me as if he was all too aware of my feelings. "I was just about to make her acquaintance."

A big smile slid across his friend's face. "Oh, I like American girls, especially ones who look like her." His stare fell from my face to the rest of me. "But what's with the uniform? Do you actually work here?" The touch of derision in his voice told me that wasn't a good thing.

"Fine!" I said, throwing up my hands. "I'll get you the stupid towels."

Both men gawked, their eyes going wide. "But," Damien began.

I didn't wait for more. Anger colored my cheeks as I stalked down the hall, only to be met by Régine from laundry, who strolled along with a cart of carefully folded white pool towels. I grabbed an armful and strode over to the men.

"Here," I said, pushing three at Damien and another two at his friend. "Wait, that's probably not enough for all your many friends." Rich, snotty friends who'd had parents looking out for them their whole lives, picking up all the bills they ran up while having their fun. "Here." I shoved five more towels at each of them. Then as Régine paused to open the pool door, I swooped up another armful and thrust them at Damien.

He scrambled to keep all the towels from falling. At least they covered up his chest, which was a good thing where my heart was concerned. Régine gaped at me with a mix of horror and fascination in her expression, and a sliver of guilt worked its way past my anger. The old woman had been here for twenty years and was probably worried about losing her job. The sliver grew to a beam—like one of the heavy-duty support beams I preferred to use in my designs.

I whirled in my flat, no-nonsense shoes and started walking away.

"Wait!" called Damien. "You didn't tell me your name."

"Yeah," his friend said with a smirk. "We *definitely* need your name."

There was no doubt why they wanted it now. I fumbled in my purse and pulled out my nametag that had just my first name. I threw it at Damien, who dropped his towels to catch it, once again leaving his gorgeous chest bare.

He was *not* yummy!

Just tell that to my heart.

I should have come to Beaumont in the winter. At least then he would have been wrapped up in a ski jacket and planning to tackle the slopes instead of strutting around half-dressed looking for pool towels.

"Make sure you get it right when you talk to the management," I said. "It's Amelia Lennox. And she"—I thumbed at

Régine, who had dived for the fallen towels—"had nothing to do with any of this."

I turned again and just about tripped over a tiny, top-heavy woman, who teetered on six-inch heels. She wore a sheer cover-up over a bikini that looked as if she'd borrowed it from Barbie's little sister—and then cut away half the material. But the honey-blond hair, dark blue eyes, and somewhat pointed face made me wonder if she was somehow related to Peter Pan. She was small enough to be his little sister. His ten-year-old sister with a pound of makeup and two obvious physical enhancements.

Her eyes rolled over me with distaste. "Really, Léandre? Hitting on the help again?" Her words came out with a refined British accent that hinted at English nobility.

"Not me," said the dark-haired man with pompous disgust. "You know me better than that, Bridgit."

I didn't wait to hear more. I stepped around the pipsqueak, noticing for the first time a tall, brown-haired girl with her. She was wearing shorts and a loose top that slid partially off one shoulder to reveal the strap on her bathing suit. Unlike Bridgit, she looked nice, and she seemed familiar, but I couldn't place her. I thought it was from the lodge, but they had so many guests here. The girl offered a fleeting smile as I hurried past.

She was probably Damien's girlfriend—unless he was with the pipsqueak. Not that I cared either way. I didn't need a man with a gorgeous chest. I didn't need *any* man. I was only here to put the past to rest once and for all. That was it.

I hurried out of the lodge through the side entrance, pretending I didn't hear Vicent from room service calling my name. He'd asked me out every day until I told him I had a boyfriend, and I didn't want to encourage him. Saying I had a boyfriend wasn't exactly a lie, because there was Emerson, and he *was* male and a friend, and if neither of us found someone else by the time we were thirty-five, we had certain plans. But for now he was the brother I'd never had, the only man I trusted.

Thankfully, Emerson was waiting for me outside the lodge on his rented motorcycle, looking hot in black leather. Hot because the sun was burning down on us, or maybe because I was still flushed. Not that he wasn't good-looking. Women said he was, and called him at all hours, hoping he'd ask them out. He had blond hair and killer green eyes, and now that the acne that had pestered him our sophomore year in college had disappeared, even I had to admit he was attractive.

Except I just didn't see him that way—and he didn't see me that way either. He could take off his shirt all day, and even though he lifted weights a couple times a week, I didn't drool over *his* chest or want to touch it.

Vicent—or someone—called after me again, but I hurtled toward Emerson. He took one look at my face and jumped from the bike, meeting me halfway. "What happened? Did you see her? How'd it go?"

"No, no. I didn't see her. Maybe she hates the place. I mean, she has a great palace to live in—why would she hang out here?"

"Well, we know the royal family owns the lodge, and all the important Beaumont families visit. It seemed logical."

I rolled my eyes. Emerson had to be the most romantic man I knew. He was almost like a woman in that respect. Still, I knew he meant well, and I had no one to blame but myself for taking his suggestion of applying for the job at the Suite Royale, wasting most of May and my entire summer here when we could have been somewhere lazing on a beach, sipping frosted drinks, and working on our tans. We deserved the rest after the grueling years in school, and it wasn't like either of us would be getting a break any time soon after we started working for real in August.

"Come on. Let's go," I said.

He looked behind me, frowning. "It is that guy from room service? I can kiss you—he's probably watching out the glass door."

I hugged Emerson then. He really was my best friend. Well, besides Harper, who had also made this trek across the ocean with me. His grip tightened. "Mel, what really happened?"

"I may have made a little bit of a scene in front of some of the guests. I think I'm going to get fired." I didn't add that it hadn't been Damien's fault. He'd only asked for towels.

Emerson drew back slightly, shaking his head. "I knew you should have taken more than just a yogurt for lunch. You're always crabby when you don't eat."

I punched him. "I am not."

He didn't let me go. "Yes, you are."

No use in arguing because he was right. "I don't even know what I'm doing here."

"Maybe you should just write her a letter. Let her know you're in town."

I snorted. "Yeah, along with all the other thousands of American girls who worship her because she has a fairy-tale life."

"Those girls aren't her sisters."

There it was. But maybe Kamille Fairbanks Lacort, whose husband, Gabriel Lacort, had recently become king of Beaumont, didn't want to meet a half sister she'd never heard of. Maybe she'd think I just wanted a piece of her fame—or worse, her husband's money.

"Please take me home," I said to Emerson.

"Okay. Just as long as you mean our cute little villa here and not America. Because I have a date tonight." He released me, throwing a leg over the bike and tossing me a helmet.

I buckled it over my chin and climbed on beside him. As I did, a movement pulled my attention to the lodge, and I looked to see Damien, his chest now disappointingly covered in a pale yellow T-shirt. Good thing I was sitting down because seeing him made my knees go all wobbly again.

Damien looked like he wanted to say something, but Emerson chose that moment to drive off. Instinctively, I pressed my face to the back of his leather jacket and held on tightly to his waist as we roared away. When we reached the end of the drive, Damien was still watching us.

I was so going to be fired.

Chapter 2

Damien

My heart was thundering, and for some reason I couldn't quite breathe—and hadn't been able to since she'd first looked up into my eyes in the hallway outside the pool door. That she watched me as the motorcycle sped out of sight should have been encouraging, but it wasn't, not with the way she was clinging to that guy. Her nametag bit into my hands where I gripped it tightly.

Amelia. The name fit her, running like sweet *miel*—honey— over my tongue.

There was something about her. Something that called to me. It wasn't only that she was the most beautiful woman I'd ever seen—with those bright blue eyes and all that dark blond hair. But something . . . more. Whether it was the fire in her amazing eyes or how she hadn't been afraid to tell me there were no towels, I couldn't say. I didn't believe in love at first sight, but I wanted to see her again.

I *needed* to see her again.

"Damien," came Stéphanie's voice from the side door of the lodge, "why'd you run off so suddenly?" That my sister was speaking English told me Bridgit was with her. Lady Bridgit Rothschild, to be exact, daughter of an English earl. The tiny pit bull, as I thought of her. It hadn't been my idea to invite her to our little vacation, but Léandre had thought it would be fun. Bridgit did know how to party, I'd give him that, but it was different this time. Maybe it had something to do with the growing unrest I'd felt ever since I'd watched Gabriel and Kami fall in love.

I turned to greet Stéphanie and Bridgit as they filed out of the lodge. Léandre was with them. "I was just trying to give this back," I said, holding up the nametag.

"She won't need it," Bridgit said with a little sniff. "Not after we report her."

Behind her Léandre smirked at me. "I agree. Even if it was a bit amusing to see you dressed in towels."

"She was off-duty," Stéphanie said. "We didn't really have a right to demand that she go searching for towels."

Léandre shook his head. "That doesn't matter. Our comfort is the bread and butter of the lodge, and we come first—if she wants to keep her job. Face it, she's just another common American, probably come here with a dream to find her prince." He rolled his eyes. "Gabriel has done more bad than good for Beaumont by marrying so far beneath himself."

That old argument again. Léandre surname was Duvauchelle, and he'd become the Baron de Accolay after his father's violent death when he was a teen. The estate was still mostly run by his domineering mother, who was very much alive, which left Léandre with too much time on his hands. In Léandre's view, his nobility made him better than the average bloke.

"We're not going to report anything," I said, tucking the

nametag into the inner mesh pocket of my swimming suit. If we get her fired, I might never see her again."

Léandre blinked at me. "Don't tell me you actually *like* the girl. She is rather attractive, but you're the Comte de Laval. You can't go slumming and expect to find anything of value, no matter what example Gabriel has set."

Léandre and I had been friends from a very young age, and we'd attended school together in England. He was there for me when my own father died of cancer in my seventeenth year. We'd been close in the nine years since, but at that moment I found I disliked him rather intensely.

Stéphanie's brown eyes flashed at Léandre. "Shut up. I think she's sweet. I met her yesterday morning in Bridgit's rooms. She must have been assigned to the English-speaking suites."

"She was in my suite?" Bridgit asked, making a face.

"She cleans it," Stéphanie's voice sounded a little strained, "so of course she was in your room. I forgot to put the do-not-disturb sign on while you were showering. She was the one who brought you fresh towels."

"Towels," I groaned. Of course, it had to be towels.

Léandre barked a laugh as he turned and pulled the lodge door open, holding it for Bridgit. "Look, if you're that attracted to the girl, go ahead and have a fling. She'd no doubt love to date a real count. Take her to your estate, show her around, have enough fun to get her out of your system—and then buy her a ticket back to America and forget her."

Bridgit's laugh trilled. "Oh, but that's too easy. Any common American girl would simply jump at that." She took Léandre's proffered arm as they began to walk down the hallway. "I'm sure she'd simply love the idea of becoming Lady Giraud. The real challenge would be if you could get her to like you without any title."

"Good idea!" Léandre said. "That way there is no expectation.

Think you've got enough in you, Damien, to woo her without your money? Let's make a wager." He and Bridgit laughed, throwing glances at me over their shoulders.

"This isn't a game." Their words unsettled me, even if I didn't want to admit it. There had been enough girls—Beaumontian and foreign—who had shown a keen interest in my title and all the money that came with it. Maybe that was even part of what had made me stick with Léandre for so long. He might rub people wrong with his blunt comments and holier-than-thou attitude, but he was quick to point out when he thought someone was trying to take advantage of me. Like the stripper who'd posed as a Spanish contessa, or the French baroness, who'd turned out to be married.

He'd been wrong about Gabriel and Kami, though. Every time I saw them together in my work for their charity, I could tell she was perfect for Gabriel. I wondered how Gabriel had felt the first time he'd seen Kami. I wondered if he could breathe.

Stéphanie touched my arm as we followed our friends down the hallway to the pool area. I glanced at her, expecting to see anger at their words, but instead, she looked thoughtful. "Damien, maybe they're right," she said in French, low enough for the others not to overhear.

"What? This from my sister who is always looking to champion those who can't speak for themselves?"

She laughed. "The girl is hardly helpless. I saw the way she threw those towels."

I stopped walking. "So you think I should try to take advantage of her?" It made me angry just thinking about it.

"No!" She punched me lightly on the arm, her freckled face wrinkling. "But if you're serious about going out with her, maybe it's better to keep who you are a secret for a while. Since you've been home running the estate this past year, you haven't been in any tabloids, and she probably won't track you down."

"Wait. You've seen her throw towels, and you still want me to lie to her?"

"Silly." Stéphanie punched me again. "It's just that . . . you're not getting any younger, and you'll need an heir."

There was that. "You talk like I'm forty, not twenty-six. There's plenty of time." I hadn't been serious about a girl in what seemed like forever, and I hadn't planned on finding a woman now, even though my mother was already hinting at how much she wanted grandchildren.

"It's to protect her as much as it is to protect you."

"How do you figure that?"

"So she can be herself around you. And so neither of you have to worry about titles or money or society. You can tell her everything once you get to know her."

"She might not even go out with me."

"She'd be crazy not to." Stéphanie leaned into me. "I just want to see you happy. And I don't care who you fall in love with, as long as whoever it is loves you as much as I do."

I put my arm around her and gave her a squeeze. "Thanks."

"Besides," she added with a laugh, "if I could get you interested in a girl, maybe you wouldn't keep scaring off all my boyfriends."

Now it was my turn to laugh. "You mean double-jointed boy, and I-still-live-with-my-mom guy? Stéphi, my sweet sister, you are better off without them."

"What do you mean? *You* still live with mom."

"The difference is that the estate is mine, so she actually lives with me. And so do you until you finish your education. At least during the summers."

"You won't scare me off. I love coming home. But I'm no different than any other girl. I want to find my prince."

I wondered if Amelia was here in Beaumont for that reason. If she was, would that be so terrible?

Inside the room that housed the indoor pool, large open windows let in both the light and the scent of the trees surrounding the lodge. I could hear splashing and laughter coming from people enjoying the outdoor pool. I'd rather be with them, but Bridgit preferred staying indoors so she didn't tan her overly pale skin, and she was so little that she was always cold in any stray breeze. Mid-May wasn't exactly summer yet in Beaumont.

Pulling off my shirt, I threw it over the stack of towels I'd tossed onto a lounge chair earlier before running after Amelia. Before I could dive into the pool, Léandre said, "Well, what's the decision? Tell you what—I won't get her fired if you can get her to go out with you. You, not the Comte de Laval." His voice had a hard edge to it that I recognized all too well. He thought he was protecting me.

I could pull rank and remind him that I was a step above him on the nobility food chain, but he'd probably push ahead anyway. "I get a week to get her to go out with me," I said. A week to get her out of my mind or to find out if there was something between us.

Léandre choked on a swallow of the drink he must have ordered from the bar while I was gone. "Three days. If it doesn't happen before then, it's not going to."

I had three days to save her job. Three days to find out why she was here in Beaumont. Three days to see if I still lost my breath around her.

I stood at the edge of the pool. "Okay," I said and dived in.

Chapter 3

Amelia

The dream came as it had in the old days when I was stressed or upset. Suddenly I was back there again, a frightened, helpless six-year-old, who'd lost her entire world.

"Don't leave me here," I whispered, clinging to my daddy's hand when he started to go down the porch stairs. "She's old and she smells funny. Daddy, please."

"You can't come where I'm going," he said, not quite looking me in the eye. His voice sounded like he was speaking through a mouthful of sand.

"I'll be good. I promise! I won't make you mad." It wasn't as if he was a good dad, but now that Mommy was dead, he was all I had.

"Look, you ain't my kid, okay?" He met my gaze then, pulling his hand away, his face twisted in anger. "She only married me because she was pregnant. Understand?"

I had no idea what that meant, and when I didn't respond fast

enough, he leaned over and put his flushed face closer to mine. "I ain't
your daddy. I never was."

Too stunned to speak, I sank to the crumbling porch and watched
him drive away in his old Ford truck. No mother. No father. And I
was left alone with a grandmother I'd never met.

As the dream faded, I lay curled in my bed, breathing hard
and biting my lip so I wouldn't cry out. I hadn't relived this dream
in several years—until coming here to Beaumont.

I'd grown up wishing I had a sister, but three months ago when
I learned I actually had one, I took it all back. Not because I didn't
long to meet her, but because it was one more secret surrounding
my life, and I was sick of secrets. Of lies. My mother's. My birth
father's. My grandmother's.

After my grandmother's death in February, I'd learned the
whole truth from a letter my birth father had written to her
shortly after his one brief visit when I was seven: I had a half sister
named Kamille Fairbanks. Then, because I was great at putting
myself into awkward situations, I'd immediately booked a flight
to Beaumont, a country I'd never heard of despite all the recent
media hype caused when their prince had married the girl who
happened to be my sister.

Instead of trying to go through proper royal chan-
nels to contact Kamille—or Kami, as she was called by most
everyone—I'd listened to Emerson's off-the-wall idea about
approaching her at the Suite Royale. At the time, telling her
privately about our connection seemed wise—the last thing I
wanted was to see my face plastered across the news. Especially
if she rejected me.

Getting the job at the lodge hadn't been a problem with its
current demand for English-speaking employees, but waiting
the months to finish my civil engineering degree at Stanford had
made it the longest three months of my life. Well, except those

months after my mother's car accident; that summer I'd lived an entire lifetime of loneliness.

"Is something wrong?" Lying in the other twin bed, Harper Thackery pushed aside dark coils of long hair and squinted at me in the sunlight filtering through our blinds.

Dragging my face from the pillow, I forced a smile. "Nothing besides the fact that I'm pretty sure I'm going to be fired today."

Harper fumbled for her phone. "Aren't you late already?"

"No, I have the late shift." I gave a jaw-cracking yawn. "I have to be there at eleven." It was my last ten-hour shift of the week, and then I had three days off. Normally, I was an early riser, but last night I'd been too worried to sleep well.

Harper rolled onto her stomach, blinking fiercely. "You know, Mel, you shouldn't be working there at all. If my grandmother died, and I found out my uncle had left her patents that were worth millions, and those patents were now all mine, I'd hire my own maid, not pretend to be one."

Like Emerson, Harper had grown up in a moderately wealthy family. I'd been the odd ball out, the girl who scraped by on scholarships and cleaning people's houses. "Oh, you know me," I said. "Frugal to a fault. Working at the lodge seemed like a good idea at the time."

"I blame your grandmother. Why that old bat let you work your fingers to the bone this past year, I'll never know. Not when she could have so easily helped you."

"I don't think she really understood about the patents. My Uncle Bryson has been dead for years, but she'd only started to receive the checks the year before she died. Besides, I told her I was on scholarship. She gave me what she could over the years."

I wasn't fooling Harper, who rolled her eyes. "No, your grandmother was an unfeeling old witch. She wasn't stupid—she knew that all the grants and good grades in the world wouldn't be enough to pay for Stanford. She let you work yourself sick because she thought it would make you a better person, even though you'd already done it for years. I bet you were the only girl at Stanford who bought all her own clothing since she was nine."

Hurt threatened to blind me with tears, but I pushed back the feelings with long practice. Grandmother hadn't been a loving person, and I had no doubt why my mother had run away as a teen, but at least the old woman hadn't abandoned me like everyone else. Yes, I'd wanted to walk away a hundred times and never see her again, but I kept coming back because by the time I'd made it to college, she couldn't cope without my weekly visits. Besides, she was the only family I had, or so I'd thought.

Harper sat up and dropped her feet to the floor. "If they don't fire you, just quit. You don't need that abuse. We'll find another way to meet your sister."

"What if she doesn't want to meet me? What if she's angry when she learns our father wasn't faithful? She was only four years old when I was born. That's not going to be easy to take. I want to know what kind of a person she is before I tell her. Because once I do that, there's no going back."

"Well, I was reading about the royal family yesterday and the only time it mentions them going to the Suite Royale is in the winter for skiing. I think you picked the wrong season."

"What about other places she might be?"

"I've been researching just that, and there is a charity ball at the palace this coming Saturday night. It's called the Children's Charity Ball because the proceeds go directly to families with children in need. Apparently, it's the first time they've held the event, and it's being sponsored and organized by none other than the queen herself. In the past they've only held a ball in the autumn that's for the daughters of the most elite—you know, debutantes. But this one targets business owners and your average rich person." Harper smirked at her own wit. "Unfortunately, all the open tickets are pre-sold so that background checks can be done, which means even if you wanted to buy one, you couldn't. And now it's by invitation only, which means people with titles who are rich enough to do whatever it takes. Too bad it's already Wednesday and you haven't run into any nobility you could tag along with. With your looks, it wouldn't have been too hard to wrangle an invitation."

I thought of Damien. I didn't know if he had connections, but his friends certainly seemed the type—not that they would want to help me, even if they knew the truth. "Last week some of the staff was bowing and scraping around and throwing out Your Ladyship and Lord Something-or-other—at least that's what I think it translated to—but I didn't notice anything this week. I don't have much time to sit and gossip, though. There do seem to be a lot of messy, spoiled rich kids who come through."

Particularly one with an incredibly gorgeous chest and a penchant for pool towels. I smiled despite myself.

"Mel!" Harper bounced from her bed, all signs of tiredness vanishing. "I know that look—what happened? Did you meet someone?"

I pushed off my quilt. "No, no, no. Well, yeah, but it's not what you think."

She grabbed the pillow from under my head. "If you don't spill, I'm going to smother you right now and send your corpse to that snotty queen."

"You don't know she's a snot."

"Tell me." Harper raised the pillow.

"Okay, okay!" I told her about the chest, his gorgeous eyes, the towels, his friends. "And did I mention his chest?" I added.

"Only three times." Harper gave a little squeal. "You have to go out with him."

"No way. He's the reason I'm going to be fired." I grabbed my phone and sprang from the bed. "Great. I have to be there in a half hour."

Harper fell back on my bed. "Amelia Lennox, you're killing me. You meet a man with a gorgeous chest and yummy eyes, and you don't even stick around to see what he has to say? I've taught you nothing over the years, have I? I have utterly failed as a roommate."

"Yummy means trouble," I said. "You taught me that."

"Those were boring American college boys, not gorgeous, rich men with sexy accents!"

"Whatever." I was too busy gathering clothes and calculating how much time I had to get to work to pay attention.

Harper popped up from my bed and grabbed my shoulders. "Okay, but promise me one thing. If you see him again, you'll at least listen to what he has to say. And if he makes your knees weak and your heart bang in your chest, you'll *do* something about it."

I stood still under her grasp. I hadn't told her that part—how my knees could barely hold my weight and how my heart threatened to leap out of my chest. "He's not for me," I said firmly. "I'm only here to see Kami. And to learn about my father. That's all." Despite my control, a tear slid down my cheek.

Harper hugged me tightly. "I'm sorry I'm so pushy. I just . . . Mel, you're the best friend I've ever had, and I want you to be happy."

"I am," I lied. I should be. I had the two greatest friends in the entire world, I'd finished my degree, I'd landed a great civil engineering job in Washington. I was going places. So why did I feel something was missing?

Stepping away from her, I grabbed the folded paper on the bedside table, a copy of my father's letter that I always had with me in case I did run into Kami. It talked about both of us and was part of the proof I'd brought to show her—if I ever got the chance. It was already looking a bit ragged, but I could always recopy the original.

"Look," I said to Harper, "you'd better go call that fiancé of yours, or he's going to wonder if you've met someone else."

Harper's expression turned soft. "Well, he's the idiot who got himself assigned to Germany with no chance of coming home for two months. He should have waited until after our wedding."

Harper went for her laptop, while I dashed from the room. The two-bedroom villa I'd rented for us had only one tiny bathroom, but it had both a tub and a shower—and the water was hot, which hadn't always been the case in the apartment I'd shared with Harper back in California. Although the villa was crammed into a community of similar villas, the area was picturesque to the point of downright cuteness. Cobblestones everywhere, little trees, and even a communal swimming pool and tennis courts. It wasn't cheap, but Emerson and Harper could be with me for no added cost. We even had wi-fi and a cute little lady named Zuleica who came in weekly to clean the house and change the bedding.

I was scarfing down three boiled eggs at the sink when Emerson came into the kitchen, still dressed in his pajamas. "Late night?" I asked. He'd gone out after bringing me home, and I hadn't heard him return.

He scratched his stomach over his shirt. "There was dancing in the street. I love Beaumont. I'm seriously thinking about moving here."

Just my luck. Harper was going to Germany after her wedding, and Emerson was threatening to stay here. "No way," I said. "You're going with me to Dickson and Company. We're going to build skyscrapers, remember?"

"Yeah, of course." He gave a huge yawn and sank down on a

chair, as I popped the last of my remaining egg into my mouth. "Any more of those left?"

I swallowed a little faster than I should have, nearly choking. "In the pan. Put them away, okay? I'm late." I snatched up my bag and ran to the door.

"You'd better take something more than a yogurt today."

"I'll grab something in the café at the lodge."

"What time do you get off? Need a ride?"

"No, I'm getting the moped back during my break. So go dance in the street some more or whatever. I'll be back at ten-thirty or so." I didn't wait for his reply.

I barely made the bus, which would put me at the lodge at 10:50 a.m. Cutting it short, but not late. As long as nothing out of the ordinary happened, I'd even have time to visit the front desk for a few minutes to see if they'd heard anything about a royal visit.

After swiping my monthly bus pass, I sank into the first available chair and began braiding my hair. Braids weren't as effective as pinning it up, but after a full day, I'd have less of a headache. As my fingers worked, I made a quick survey of the bus, which was mostly full of tourists and Beaumontian women carrying baskets of food. Many of the mature native women wore black, and I wondered who they mourned. For a stark moment, I felt the old ache left by my mother's passing.

When the bus let me off at the bottom of the drive leading up to the lodge, I had already seesawed a dozen times about what would be waiting for me. In one scenario, I'd be fired, and in the other, I'd be given a stern warning. I hoped it wasn't too bad, or the clerks at the front desk wouldn't spill any news about visiting royals. If only I'd been assigned there in the first place instead of cleaning rooms.

I'd barely walked into the breakroom to clock in when Régine came up to me. "Good morning," she said in heavily accented English, "someone left flowers for you. They at front desk."

"For me?" I blinked at her suspiciously. A gift of flowers might be how they fired their employees here; it was an upscale lodge, after all. I looked around to see at least a dozen of my fellow employees watching me, most smiling encouragingly. So maybe flowers didn't mean I was being fired.

"Really," Régine said. Leaning closer, she whispered, "Maybe from that man yesterday?"

"Not a chance," I retorted, barely holding in a snort. When she looked at me blankly, I smiled. "Uh, thanks. Front desk?"

At least that fell into my plan to pump the employees there for information. I'd have to work harder to finish my assigned rooms on time, but I was willing to do that.

At the front desk, I waited until Pierre wasn't busy. He was nicer than Benedetta, the other clerk, and always willing to practice his English with me. "Hey, Régine said someone left flowers."

Pierre laughed. "Yes, just a minute." He winked and went into the back room, returning almost instantly with a huge vase of flowers of every type and color. It was too much—far too much—and so of course I loved them instantly.

Pierre's voice lowered. "Someone really likes you, no?"

Or someone really wanted something. "I guess so." I glanced to either side, but no one seemed to be staring at me. "Who are they from?" I asked.

Pierre jutted his chin forward, indicating the lobby behind me, the one place I hadn't looked. "Him."

Oh, no. I turned to see the guy from yesterday standing up from one of the couches near the dormant fireplace. His grin was wide, and if anything, he was better looking than I remembered. My knees started that wobbly thing again, and my breath caught in my throat as he began to cross the lobby toward me. Today, Damien was fully dressed, but he gave a new, heart-stopping style to casual slacks and button-down shirts.

"I have to get to work," I muttered, swinging around to face Pierre. "I haven't clocked in."

Pierre rolled his eyes. "It will wait. For now, you have to talk to Lor—uh him."

"Wait, about the royal family. Any word?"

Pierre looked beyond me to Damien, as if he wanted to say something, but nothing came out. Finally, he shook his head. "No word. Sorry. They aren't coming." So their private rooms would remain vacant for at least the days I would be off. I didn't know whether to be happy or weep with frustration.

Apparently, I couldn't do either, because Pierre was jerking his head, indicating for me to turn around again. I took a deep breath and rotated—and nearly ran into Damien a second time. There was no way I could pretend not to see him.

Damien nodded at Pierre, who ducked his head and stared at us with a gleam in his dark eyes. I took a couple steps away from the desk, my hands shaking so much that I hoped I didn't drop the heavy vase. Why couldn't he be ugly? Or at least unappealing to me? It would make this so much easier.

"So," Damien said in his incredibly sexy accent, "I wanted to apologize for yesterday."

"Uh, thanks." Then honesty forced me to add, "But I was the one who"—I glanced at Pierre and lowered my voice—"threw towels at you."

Damien dipped his head in an incredibly adorable way. "Yeah, but you were off duty; I should have been more observant. I guess I was noticing other things."

His golden eyes held mine as he spoke, and my heart threatened to beat right out of my chest. Did he mean what I thought he meant? Then I shook myself mentally. It didn't matter. I wasn't here for fun; I had to focus on my purpose here, my quest.

"Well, thanks," I said, backing farther away from both him and the desk, staggering slightly under the weight of the flowers. I was glad I'd left my purse in my locker, or I'd be even more awkward.

"Wait." He stepped closer, preventing me from turning away. "I brought this for you." He held out my name tag on the palm of his hand.

"Oh, right. Thanks." I juggled the flowers as I took it from him.

"I'd like to take you to dinner, if you have time." When he smiled, his right cheek dimpled. Not that I was noticing.

"Thanks, but no," I said. "It was really my fault. I hadn't eaten, and I get a little crank—" Ugh, why was I telling him that? "Anyway, it was my fault. I'm really sorry."

"Please, I'd like to." He moved closer. If he took another step, he'd no doubt be able to smell the egg on my breath. Not a lovely image I wanted to keep with me all afternoon.

I inched away. "Look, you're nice, but I'm not . . . I think it's better that we just leave it at this."

"Why?"

"Because I'm not interested." I couldn't quite meet his gaze as I told the lie.

"In food?" He laughed. "No wonder you were so cranky yesterday."

Guess I wasn't fooling him. Flushing, I took a step back, stumbling slightly. His arm shot out to steady me, sending a jolt throughout my body like something from a torrid romance novel. What had I been saying? Oh, right. "I mean I'm not interested in a relationship. I'm only here for a few months."

His hand dropped, but his smile remained. "I see. But you still need to eat." He raised his hands. "You could have dinner with me with—how do you Americans call it?—no strings attached? Just for an apology."

Yes, I wanted to say. But there was this whole rock band going on inside my chest whenever I looked at him, and I had a career ahead of me back in America. Band or no, I wasn't about to leave my heart here in Beaumont. At least not any more of it than was already with its queen. "Sorry. I have to pick up my rental vehicle on my break, and I don't get off work until ten. Everything near here is closed. Even the lodge restaurant closes before then."

"Well, I know a little Italian restaurant just down the street. It serves the best minestrone in Beaumont, and the lasagna is to die for." He gave me another brilliant smile.

"Papa Amorosi's?" I felt myself wavering. I'd walked past it before, but I hadn't had the time to go in yet. The smells coming out of the place were almost enough for me to live on.

"You'll love it. I'll meet you here, and we'll walk together."

He was gone before I could kick myself. I'd learned at Stanford that you never, ever give an excuse if you don't want to date a guy. You just say you aren't interested, and then follow that up with a big fat no. And another, if necessary. I'd never had to say no more than three times. Somehow none of that preparation had worked here.

Maybe because I hadn't wanted to say no.

On the bright side, I'd get a free meal at a restaurant I'd been wanting to try, and I hadn't been fired. There were more days than I could count in my past when those two things alone would have been enough to celebrate. I might be worth five million dollars now, but in my heart I was still an impoverished, scraping-by, barely-able-to-feed-myself, parentless student.

I retraced my steps to the employee lounge, knowing I was going to clock in late. But Régine was there, and she waved me away from the time cards. "I already passed it through. Here, give to me." She tugged the flowers from my grasp and set them on the nearest table. "Just remember to take home later."

I most certainly wouldn't be taking them anywhere. Even if I could get them home on my moped, I didn't need questions from Harper and Emerson. I had enough questions for all of us. Still, as I hurried to get my cleaning cart, I didn't dread the day as much as I had before. I wondered if I'd like minestrone.

Chapter 4

Damien

I knew the flowers were a mistake the minute she had them in her arms—they were too much. Why hadn't I picked something smaller? She was maybe a little on the taller side for a woman, but with the water, that vase must have been heavy. Somehow, she'd made it down the hall without dropping them.

At least she'd agreed to eat dinner with me—well, sort of. I had twisted her arm. But I couldn't feel too bad about it because I knew I hadn't imagined the pull between us.

Unfortunately, I had just invited her to eat at a restaurant I knew stopped serving at ten on the weekend, and that meant they'd close at least an hour earlier tonight. But I hadn't wanted to take her to just any loud bar on the street, even if those near the Suite Royale were classier than most.

So I needed to visit Papa Amorosi's and fix things for tonight.

At least Amorosi knew who I was, and with the right incentive, he'd do me the favor of staying open.

"Damien!"

I glanced up to see my sister waving at me. She was alone, and I was relieved not to have to answer Léandre and Bridgit's inevitable questions. Getting Amelia—or *Miel,* as I thought of her—to agree to have dinner with me as a friend didn't really count as a date. I waited for my sister to catch up.

"How'd it go?" she asked.

"Well, we're going to dinner tonight."

Stéphanie pumped her fist. "Great!"

"I don't know. She turned me down at first. It's just as friends. And it's awkward trying to talk to her here. I'm afraid at any moment the clerks at the desk are going to Your Lordship this or Your Lordship that."

"Too bad we can't invite her to our place."

I laughed. "Oh, right. Come to my huge estate. And, no, I'm not really a count."

"Well, there's always the cottage. Mother's there now." Stéphanie gave me a happy smile. The cottage was on our property but was rather small as houses went. Quaint, most people called it. Our parents had stayed at the cottage when they wanted to be alone with no servants around, and we'd spent many weekends there as children.

"Amelia is working here, so it's not like she can up and leave on a whim. Besides, I barely convinced her to go to Papa Amorosi's with me."

"Well, a girl can dream."

Her laugh reminded me of my mother's. We probably should have gone with her to the cottage this week, instead of coming to the lodge with our friends. I was finding there wasn't as much attraction in Léandre's party scene as there had once been. But if I'd gone to the cottage, I wouldn't have met Miel.

"I can drop you off at the cottage on the way back to the estate," I said.

"You won't come?"

I frowned. "Probably not. Julien is a good manager, but I need to oversee the upgrades in the north factory."

Stéphanie frowned at something over my shoulder. "Oh, there's Bridgit. I promised I'd go shopping with her."

"Again?"

She laughed. "The Children's Charity Ball is Saturday, remember? I have the dress, of course, but I'm looking for the perfect tiara, and as much as I hate to say it, Bridgit knows where to find the best. She's got a nose for it, I think. Now hurry and get out of here. Don't look back. She hinted this morning that you weren't having enough fun and that we needed to take you with us. I think she might be deciding to go after you, if you know what I mean. She wouldn't stop questioning me last night about who you might be dating. For real, that is. She doesn't count Amelia."

Stifling a groan, I leaned over and kissed my sister's cheeks, then practically ran for the door.

On the way to Papa Amorosi's, I thought about our conversation. Before my old manager had died last year, my greatest endeavors in life had been finishing college, representing our family for Gabriel's charity, and tearing up the town with Léandre. But last year I'd decided it was time to take over running my own estate and our olive oil factories.

My decision had pleased my mother, and for that alone it had been worth it, but to my surprise, I discovered I was good at business and enjoyed the work. It was far more rewarding than going to bars and balls and other functions and having the media tell lies about what you'd been doing. The past year had been grueling, like a crash course in business, but the growth of my company had been worth it. In fact, I'd been thinking of finding some excuse to leave this little vacation and return to work.

Until I'd seen Miel.

*E*yes followed me through the lobby. Apparently the clerks from this morning had filled in the next shift of workers about the flowers and my attention to Miel. I hoped they'd also passed on the directions not to call me Your Lordship or any such nonsense, but I couldn't depend on that, so I planned to stay far away.

I settled in the lobby to wait for Miel. I'd changed into dark pants and a gray- and black-pinstriped, long-sleeved shirt, but I realized now, as I watched one of the maids cleaning the windows, that I should have remained in my regular clothes. Miel would probably be dressed in her uniform, and I'd only make her feel uncomfortable.

Yet when Miel finally appeared ten minutes later, the sight of her made me catch my breath. She wasn't wearing the uniform at all, but a swirly, sleeveless, multi-colored dress that made me think of a woman standing on a bluff above an ocean as the wind blew around her. Her blond hair added to the imagery, hanging past her shoulders, freed from the braid she'd worn earlier. Thankfully, my flowers were nowhere to be seen.

My mouth suddenly felt dry. *She's leaving in a few months,* I warned myself.

I didn't care.

I crossed the space between us, and her smile nearly did me in. I wanted to lean over and taste her lips—just once, but that would probably scare her off. "You look beautiful." I forced my hand to stay at my side. Sometimes Léandre and I would make a show of kissing ladies' hands at balls and other events we'd had to attend since our teen years—frankly, since we'd started liking girls, that was always the most interesting part of the evening—but this was different somehow.

Miel laughed, and it sounded like the wind running through the chimes outside the cottage. Like coming home. "I know how stunning you think the uniforms are here, but I was sick of wearing it."

"I only like them because they match your eyes." I nearly bit my tongue after saying it because I was quite certain friends didn't say such things. At least she'd know from the beginning that I wanted more. Because I was pretty certain I did want a lot more.

I gestured toward the door before she could change her mind. "Shall we?" This close, I could see that beneath the bright smile she was tired. Who wouldn't be after a ten-hour workday? Well, at least I could make sure she got off her feet and ate a decent meal.

The evening wasn't too cold, but it might be in an hour when we left the restaurant, and I contemplated stopping off at my car for a jacket to loan her later. But not everyone drove a new convertible, and though I hadn't told Léandre I'd pretend to be a complete pauper, letting her see the car seemed risky since she hadn't agreed to a real date yet. Amelia's nervous expression solved the matter, and I opted to leave the jacket in the car.

"So," I said as we strolled down the street. "What brings you to Beaumont?"

"What, you mean besides dreaming I'll find and marry a prince?"

Something bitter curled inside me. "Is that why you're here? To find a prince?"

She laughed and rolled her eyes. "Please, I think that's been done. No, I . . ." She paused, as if deciding how much to tell me.

"Well, school was over, and I needed a break. My friends and I came here to see the country. You know, it's been in the news a lot lately."

"Yeah, it's actually been good for the economy. I work at an olive oil factory, and we've increased our output twenty-five percent. It's been a good year."

"Olive oil? Really? That's great."

"We Beaumontians love our olive oil."

"So do I. Especially on salads the way you guys serve it with vinegar and salt."

"Good. You'll eat our brand tonight. Papa Amorosi is one of our customers." Our hands brushed as we stepped down from the cobbled sidewalk and crossed the street. A spark of something shot up my arms and over my shoulders.

"So tell me more about you," I said. "You mentioned school. Are you studying?"

"Isn't this the restaurant?"

"Oh, right." I'd almost walked right past. I could have walked forever at her side.

True to his word, Amorosi's grandson had the lights on and the closed sign off. He would also have someone near the door, turning away anyone who might wander inside. I opened the door for Miel before she could reach for it, and sure enough, a waitress was at the door. She welcomed us in Italian, and as she showed us to a table, I glanced back to see Amorosi's grandson flipping over the closed sign and locking the door.

Candles lit the table where the waitress seated us. "It's almost as if they were waiting for us," Amelia murmured. "I thought they closed earlier." She looked over the menu. "Okay, this is all in Italian with French translations. I can only read a little."

"Will you allow me to order?" I asked.

She appeared relieved. "Sure."

"Anything in particular you like?"

"I like everything."

I turned to the waitress and ordered a *crostino* assortment for the appetizer, to be followed by half portions of minestrone, with lasagna and a side salad just in case. "With plenty of your fresh bread," I added. In my experience, Americans loved our bread.

"So," I said when we were alone. "You were saying about school?"

Her face came alive and her tiredness vanished as she told me about graduating from Stanford University with a degree in civil engineering and the promising job that awaited her in Washington. Even I'd heard of Stanford, and the idea of her studying there fit my perception of her personality much better than her cleaning at the Suite Royale.

Her love of the business was obvious as she talked about materials, creative manipulation, and the scientific ideas involved in making a structure safe for a certain load. I loved how much she loved it; I could feel her passion, and I fell a little bit more for her with every word and gesture. "I can tell you like building things," I said when she paused to take a breath.

She leaned forward, her eyes holding mine. "Not just building anything, but things that will stand forever." She laughed and sat back. "Or close to it. I especially love working on tall buildings and bridges. And I have to admit, I took a lot of architectural design classes as well. I didn't want to build ugly structures."

Not that anything could be ugly with her heart and soul in it. "So, working at the lodge," I prompted.

She shrugged, her smile faltering. "Think of it as life experience. I've never been out of the country before, and it was a way to do that without incurring a lot of expense. It's how I earned money for college—though mostly I worked in private homes."

"What about family?" I regretted the question immediately when her expression turned carefully blank.

"My mother died when I was six from untreated pneumonia. She thought it would pass, and by the time she got to the hospital, it was too late." Her voice was stiff, and I understood because I still mourned my own father. "I went to live with my grandmother. She, uh, wasn't exactly the kind of grandmother who makes cookies and gives you hugs. I'd be lying if I didn't say it was a little bit of a relief when she died earlier this year." The blank expression became a sad smile, and I knew she regretted the truth. "But while she was alive, my mother was the best mother a little girl could have. She always hugged me and played with me. She did a lot of things wrong, but not where I was concerned, and I always knew she loved me."

I wanted to ask what kind of things her mother had done wrong, but instead I asked, "No siblings? And your father?"

She shook her head. "My father's dead too."

"I'm sorry."

"Don't be. I only met him once. I didn't even learn the man we'd been living with wasn't my real father until my mother died."

I was curious about the details, but her eyes avoided mine—a sure sign she didn't want to talk about it. More than anything, I wanted to take her mind from her past, so I told her about my father and how lost I'd felt when he'd died. "My mother was a rock, though," I added. "And I have a great sister."

"Then we were both lucky," she said with a determination that seemed forced.

Thankfully the waitress chose that moment to arrive with our appetizer. "Ah, these are called 'little toasts,'" I explained to Miel, "and we eat them with cheese and meats and many other toppings. I hope you're hungry. I ordered a variety."

"Actually, I'm starving."

She was. Together we finished every one, and by then they had served the minestrone. We hadn't made it halfway through that when they brought the lasagna and the salads. Miel's laughter warmed the quiet restaurant. "I'll see you the minestrone and raise you half a lasagna." She wrinkled her nose. "But, seriously, I don't think I can eat it all."

"Well, let's give it a shot." I liked seeing her eat.

She dipped a piece of bread in the olive oil, clove, and vinegar mixture that came with the meal. "You weren't lying about this being the best olive oil in the world. I'll have to take home a bottle."

"I'll bring you one."

For a moment neither of us said anything, and I realized my comment indicated that we would see each other again. Everything had been so natural between us that I hadn't even considered the comment before I spoke. The idea of *not* seeing her again was impossible.

After a few more minutes of casual conversation and intermittent chewing, she tossed down her napkin. "I'm finished. I can't eat another bite."

"Neither can I." I didn't want the night to end, but what could I do? I gave my credit card to the waitress, and all too soon she was back, and Miel and I were walking out into the decidedly cooler night. The street was almost deserted.

Amelia rubbed her arms, and I wished I had that jacket to offer her now.

"Are you working tomorrow?" I asked, keeping my voice casual. If she shot me down, I didn't plan on giving up. Some things were worth fighting for, and tonight had only shown me that I needed more of her.

"Actually, I have the next three days off."

I blinked. If that wasn't fate stepping in, I didn't know what fate was. "That's great!"

I moved around in front of her and began walking backward so I could see her face. "My sister was saying earlier how she wanted to go home and visit my mom. I'd love for you to come with us so I can show you the countryside."

"Oh, I couldn't. I'm here with friends." Was it me or was her refusal reluctant?

Mother had been urging me to find a wife. Now that I was overseeing the business, she'd mostly retired, and the hints about me settling down came more frequently. There had never been anyone I could see bringing home to her, but I wanted to take Miel now.

I stumbled over a jutting cobblestone, and she laughed at my windmilling arms. "Besides, I don't even know your last name."

My full name was Damien Bellecourt Romain Frédéric Giraud, and an Internet search would tell her I was the Count of Laval, so that was a problem if I wanted to keep my nobility a secret—which I'd only have to do until I knew if she liked me. But I could give at least one of my names.

"I'm Beaumontian," I said. "I have a million names: both my grandmothers' maiden names and my mother's maiden name. My mother would have tacked on more, if my father had let her. But you can just call me Damian Bellecourt. And your friends are invited to come. The house isn't very large, but we have an extra room or two."

She stopped walking and so did I. Her fantastic eyes looked almost black in the moonlight, and I wanted to kiss her more than I'd ever wanted to kiss a woman. I wasn't entirely sure how I felt about that because if she kissed me back, it would prove she liked me and not my title.

But somehow it also felt a lot like lying.

Chapter 5

Amelia

*I*f my chest pounded any harder, Damien was going to hear it. I wanted him to kiss me more than I'd wanted just about anything. Well, except maybe that my mother was still alive. I hadn't felt this way ever, though I'd kissed more than my fair share of boys during high school when I'd been searching for . . . what? I still didn't know.

Damien was Beaumontian, and there could be nothing between us. Could there? I'd already spilled more of my guts to him during the past ninety minutes than I'd told anyone besides Harper and Emerson. Now that I thought about it, I felt vulnerable.

I looked away, breaking our connection. "I don't know. I'd have to ask my friends what they want to do." Actually, I would love to go with Damien and his sister, to see more of Beaumont than this little section around the lodge. I took a step forward, and he turned to walk with me, his face sober instead of teasing.

"You're shivering." His arm reached tentatively around my

shoulders. It had been a dumb idea wearing this dress that Régine had rescued from the lost and found bin that was destined for charity, but she'd convinced me I couldn't go out with Damien in my uniform—not that it was a real date. I'd made that perfectly clear.

It felt like a real date, though.

His arm beneath his long sleeve was warm against my bare skin, and I let myself sink against him. "Where does your mom live?" I asked.

"In a little city called Laval." He hesitated before adding, "So will you talk to your friends? Stéphanie and I have a thing we have to go to Saturday night, but I'm sure you'll find plenty to do without us. You can stay for as long as you want."

"I'll talk to my friends, and see what they say."

"Good."

We walked a while longer before I said, "But I don't want you to think . . . I'm not the kind of girl who . . ."

He held up his hands, his humor returning. "Hey, my mother is going to be there."

I laughed. "You still live with your mother?"

"Not exactly. The house—it's a cottage, really—is hers, and I have my own place. But the truth is, we spend a lot of time together. Since my father died, Stéphanie and I are all she has. We're really close."

Now I wanted to go more than ever. I'd never seen a functional family in action. I'd been to Harper's house once or twice over the years, but she was an only child and her parents were rarely home by the time she came into my life. Emerson's parents were uncivilly divorced, and both of them were attorneys who worked seventy hours a week. Then there was my grandmother. All of that felt so different from the love in Damien's voice when he spoke about his mother—that was something I wanted to see.

I didn't fool myself into thinking my mother would have been like that, if she'd lived, but maybe she would have quit her parties and her sleeping around. I'd never know.

"You've gone quiet all of a sudden," Damien said.

I looked up at him, realizing we were already back at the lodge. "Oh, sorry. I was just thinking."

"Penny for your thoughts? Isn't that how you say it?"

"Yes, but my thoughts are worth far more than a penny." I forced a laugh. "Well, it looks like this is it. Thank you for dinner. I had fun."

"I'd like to walk you to your car. It's a pretty safe area, but it's dark."

I agreed, so he waited until I went inside for my things—minus the flowers, which would have to stay in the breakroom—and then walked with me to where I'd parked my rental moped. "Wait," he said, "you're driving home on that. In the dark? In a dress?"

His expression made me laugh. "You think I can't?"

"No, I think it sounds incredibly fun. Will that thing hold two? I'd love a night ride—just to see you home."

"How will you get back?"

"Don't worry. I'll call someone to pick me up." His stare sent a warmth through me that made me almost forget I was cold. "Please?"

"Okay."

I stowed my belongings in the compartment under the seat and started the moped. He climbed on the back, and I perched on the edge of the seat. But the space between us vanished as his arms went around me, pulling me back against his very firm chest. My breath caught in my throat. *So not a good idea.*

I drove through the quiet streets, the whine of the moped loud in my ears. Wind rushed past. I laughed, loving the adrenaline even this low speed gave me—or was it his touch? He held me tighter around the turns, and I found myself taking roads and detours I'd never taken before. Even so, we pulled up at my housing development all too soon.

"You live kind of far away from the lodge, don't you?" he asked.

"Not really," I admitted. "I took the long way."

He grinned at that. "I'm glad. It was fun. Give me the address, and I'll text my sister to pick me up."

"Won't she mind?"

"Not when she learns I'm taking her to see our mother." He paused before adding, "Especially if you agree to come with me."

I laughed. "You don't give up, do you?"

"No. I don't." Just a simple phrase, but it felt like a promise.

Leaving the moped in front of my villa, I walked to one of the benches on the curving pathway that snaked through the area, connecting all the little houses. He followed me, but not before I saw him glance at the villa, as if wondering why I didn't want to invite him in to see my friends.

And why don't you? I wondered. Maybe because I still wasn't sure.

His phone vibrated. "Looks like Stéphanie's on her way," he said.

We'd barely sat on the bench when Emerson and Harper drove up on his bike. They were off in a second and coming in our direction. So much for keeping them apart. Rising to meet them, I made quick introductions and told them about dinner, noting the way Damien sized up Emerson, who chose to stand close enough to me that our arms brushed. If I wanted, I could lean into Emerson, and he'd chase Damien away like he had every guy I'd wanted to get rid of for the past three years. But I didn't want to get rid of Damien.

"So," Damien said, "these are your friends."

I suspected he'd thought my "friends" were both women, and he wasn't sure what to make of the fact that one of them was the man who'd picked me up yesterday at the hotel.

"Best friends for the past three years," Emerson said, taking off his black leather jacket and placing it around my shoulders. Warmth cradled my body, and I nodded at him thankfully. "Well, three for me and Mel," Emerson continued, "and four for her and Harper. I graduated from the same engineering program as Mel, and we're heading to work for the same company in August."

"I see." Damien's words were strained, and for some inexplicable reason it gave me a little thrill to see that he was jealous of Emerson. Harper would tease me to no end if I confessed such a childish reaction.

After a heartbeat, Damien plunged on. "We were just talking about you two. I invited, uh, Mel—and both of you—to visit my mother's cottage and see some of the countryside for a few days. We have access to bicycles and horses, if you want them."

"You have horses?" I asked. He hadn't mentioned that. No one I knew growing up could afford a horse—just how well off was his family? The idea made me uncomfortable for reasons I couldn't begin to name.

"They belong next door, but you're free to use them. I could also take you to an olive oil factory if you're interested. And the groves where they grow the trees."

Harper squealed, making Damien jump. "That sounds absolutely fabulous! Let's do it. What do you say, Emerson?"

Emerson looked back and forth between Damien and Harper for a moment before his eyes came to rest on my face. "Well?"

I could see he wanted to. Maybe dancing in the street was getting old. I transferred my gaze to Damien. "Will those friends of yours from the hotel be there?"

"No. Unless you want them to be." One side of his mouth quirked upward in a hesitant half-smile.

"Uh, I'll pass on them."

"But you'll go?" Damien looked almost like a little boy begging for a treat, and both of my friends silently awaited my response.

I couldn't disappoint any of them. Or myself. "Okay. I'd love to."

Damien was grinning fully now. "Great. We'll come by and get you in the morning."

"Yippee!" shouted Harper. "I'm going to pack." She hurried off toward the villa, her dark hair streaming after her.

Damien stood looking pointedly at Emerson, who didn't take the hint. Instead, Emerson sat down on the bench and leaned back. "Your country is a bit chilly at night, but the stars up here are so clear."

"They're even brighter near our cottage," Damien said, speaking more to me than to Emerson. "Not so many houses. And it'll get warmer in another month." His look seared me, and I wished I could kick Emerson into the villa so we could be alone. Maybe one kiss wouldn't be so bad.

I was trying to think of something to respond to Damien, or a way to get rid of Emerson, when a sleek convertible drove down the street. "That's my ride," Damien said. "Guess I'll see you tomorrow."

I was going to kill Emerson.

Then again, maybe he'd saved me from myself.

Damien's sister turned out to be the nice-looking girl from the incident at the lodge, who spoke with the same British accent he used. Damien made brief introductions, and in the next minute, he slid into the driver's seat, and they drove off.

Emerson's hand fell on my shoulder as I watched them disappear. "You okay?"

"Yeah."

"He seems nice."

"He is."

Emerson's eyes fell to my lips, and I recognized the signs. Sometimes it was him and sometimes it was me, but every now and then we had to go through this. He gently turned me around and brought his lips to mine. He was warm and smelled nice, but that was all. No fireworks.

He sighed. "Just checking."

I leaned against him. "It would be so much easier, wouldn't it?"

"But you're still having my baby in twelve years if neither of us get married, right?"

"Of course." We'd made the pact last year after a serious discussion about children, which we both wanted. With the tragedy of my mother's life and the disaster of his parents' divorce, neither of us had much faith in falling passionately in love. At least our friendship was something that would last.

He put an arm around me. "Come on. Let's go pack. How rich is this guy anyway? That car was nice."

"Not too, I don't think. Anyone can make payments on a nice car."

"What about staying at the lodge? That's pricey."

"He said something about staying in his friend's suite."

"Too bad. Then don't tell him anything about your inheritance. The last thing you need is a gold digger. Promise?"

I laughed. "I promise."

As we walked back to the villa, he said, "You know, the nicest thing about this Damien of yours is that he has a really hot sister."

Damien

"Aren't you ready yet, Stéphi?" I asked through the door of Stéphanie's room in the three-bedroom suite we shared with Léandre.

The door opened. "It's only seven! Why are we leaving so early? Will Amelia and her friends even be awake?"

"I wanted to buy her this thing I saw in the gift shop yesterday. Did you tell Mom we were coming?"

"I texted her last night, and she called me this morning while I was still in bed. She's getting everything ready."

"Did you tell her about not mentioning my title and not having any servants there?"

"Yeah, and she was thrilled enough about you bringing *any* girl home that she agreed not to say anything—but she also made it a point to tell me she isn't going to lie."

"I know. Let's just see how it goes the first day."

"I think you've won your bet with Léandre, haven't you? I know I said you shouldn't tell her, but now I'm not so sure anymore."

"I'm right about protecting him," Léandre said from the doorway of his room. He was still dressed in pajama bottoms and a white shirt, his dark hair sticking out oddly on one side. "Besides, why tell her at all if this is just a little fling?" His dark eyes glinted. "Have you kissed her yet?"

I felt a lot of things for Miel, but fling didn't describe any of them. "Look," I told him, "whatever deal you think we had—it's off. I like her and she likes me."

Léandre frowned for a few seconds, but then he nodded. "Okay, but be careful, man."

I will. I had to be. Becoming involved with the wrong woman could be an emotional and financial disaster. Thousands of workers depended on me to keep food on their tables, and I didn't take that responsibility lightly.

"Although," Léandre drawled, "you might want to rethink your relationship with Bridgit. She may have a thing for you."

Stéphanie rolled her eyes. "That's only because he's interested in Amelia. Bridgit hates the idea of any noble being attracted to a commoner."

I pushed inside Stéphanie's room to get her suitcase. I'd had more than enough conversation about Bridgit. She'd once had her claws out for Gabriel, with the idea of being Beaumont's queen, and when that failed, she'd started working her way down the nobility chain. Maybe she'd finally wake up one day and realize that Léandre was in love with her and had been since we were all in school back in England. I didn't know whether to laugh at the irony or to feel sorry for him.

A knocking at the door told me the porter had arrived. He carried out our suitcases while we said goodbye to Léandre. "See you Saturday night," he said. "But call me if you need help getting rid of this girl." The calculating look in his eyes told me he wasn't joking.

"Maybe you should come and get to know her." I regretted the offer the minute it left my lips. Miel had made it clear she didn't want him, and I had no desire to share her with anyone else—and especially not him.

Léandre arched a brow. "If you were staying at your estate, then maybe Bridgit and I would come, but the cottage has nothing but acres of trees and hills. I think we're better off here. You know how Bridgit loves to shop."

"I do, indeed." Thankfully, I'd dodged that bullet, but I couldn't help feeling a little sorry for my friend.

Stéphanie and I followed the porter downstairs, where I ducked into the gift shop. I'd seen a 3D puzzle there of the Beaumontian palace that I thought she might enjoy building. I knew it wasn't the same thing as designing one yourself, but she might like it once she was back in the States.

Just thinking of her leaving made me feel melancholy. But that didn't make sense. Two days ago I hadn't noticed anything missing from my life, and now all I could think about was being with her. I'd changed a lot since my last few poor decisions about women, but could I trust my judgment now where Amelia was concerned?

My phone rang while the porter and the valet were placing the luggage into the trunk of my convertible. I recognized the number, and I wasn't surprised to see who was calling. "Hi, Kami," I said.

Technically, I should have called her "Your Royal Highness," but we never used titles between us. Léandre and I hadn't exactly been kind to her when she'd first caught Gabriel's attention, but I'd tried to make it up to her this past year. Kami and I had a lot of contact because of the charity, and I liked to think we'd become friends.

"Hey, Damien. I guess you know why I'm calling."

A few weeks ago I might have said something like, "Because you want to leave Gabriel and find a real man like me," and she would have laughed. But that felt odd now, with my head full of Miel. "Your first Children's Charity ball," I said. "Yes, Stéphi and I will be there. We're even trying to convince my mother to come. She doesn't get out much these days."

"Oh, I'd love to see her." Kami paused a few seconds before rushing on. "I have to confess, I'm a little nervous. This is the first event that I'm completely in charge of."

"So that's why you've called three times this month."

She laughed. "Well, it's important that all of the nobles be there. Many of the businessmen are only coming because they'll have a chance to rub shoulders with all of you."

"We'll be there."

"Even Léandre?" Reluctance entered her voice.

"No need to call him," I said, slipping the porter and the valet a tip. "He'll be there."

"Oh, I usually make Gabriel call him, but he'll be glad not to."

I wanted to tell her not to be too hard on Léandre, but she had every reason to be—for now. Still, people could change. I had.

"Well, thanks, Damien. Tell Stéphanie I'm looking forward to seeing her."

"I will."

We said goodbye, and I slipped into the driver's seat of my convertible next to my sister, who was already inside. "Kami again?" Stéphanie asked. "She shouldn't be so nervous. She always thinks of everything. If it's so hard for her, she could always assign you to plan the next event."

"Yeah, yeah," I murmured, putting the car into gear. In ten minutes I'd see Miel.

"You didn't even hear me!" Stéphanie glanced over, a wide

smile on her face. "You must really like this girl, because we both know you'd make a horrible mess of any fundraiser."

She was right on both accounts. I hadn't been able to sleep, breakfast had tasted like cardboard, and I couldn't think about anything but Miel. Not that I would tell my little sister that.

I slammed my foot on the gas. "I don't know what you're talking about."

Amelia

*D*amien was the perfect gentleman, taking my backpack stuffed with only the bare essentials and also reaching for my hand. The moment he touched me, the world stopped. In that instant, there was only him and me. No one else. I wanted . . . wanted . . . I didn't know what I wanted, but it involved him. I hadn't even thought about Kami all night, or what I would say to her once I met her.

"Top up or down?" Damien asked as he opened the door to his convertible.

"Down!" Harper and I said together. Our hair would be a tangled mess, but it would be worth it.

I loved the way the car hugged the road and took the curves, and I admired how Damien pointed out highlights as we passed. "Those ruins over there were left by the Romans," he said. "Or at least they're behind the piles of dirt you're seeing. City officials found the Roman ruins during an attempted remodel of an old building that was apparently built on top, and now they're excavating them. Want to see?"

We stopped and took pictures, and though the ruins themselves weren't very impressive, that might have been because my attention was completely occupied by Damien.

Afterwards we bought *gelato,* and while we finished our cold treats, he drove us to a bluff that overlooked a valley, where we climbed from the car to admire the scenery.

"It's beautiful," I said, gazing at small hills and trees, bright green with spring growth. "What is this place?" I asked.

"It's Laval. Our city." There was pride in his voice, and it evoked the strangest response inside my chest. I'd never felt the way he did about anywhere I'd lived. Mostly, I'd looked forward, wanting to escape, but if I'd come from a city like this, maybe I would have had a place to love and would never want to leave.

"Come on." He glanced at the others as he took my hand, pulling me along the bluff. "There's something I want to show you."

We walked for a few minutes until our friends were swallowed by the trees. We rounded a thick clump, and the view opened even wider to reveal an enormous building in the distance that seemed to be half manor and half castle. It was surrounded by luscious gardens and trees and large expanses of grass. Beyond the manor, groves of trees filled the horizon.

"Olive trees," Damien said. "And over there—far over there—you see that building?" His arm slipped around me, pulling me close and pointing to the left near a settlement of houses. "That's one of the olive oil factories."

"It's all so . . . peaceful."

"I used to come up here with my father on horseback. He loved this view as much as I did." Again, his tone told me exactly how much he loved it.

"I can see why."

I wet my lips with my tongue and looked up to find him watching me. I knew before his face moved toward mine what he was going to do. I didn't move away. His lips touched mine, tenderly at first, gently exploring. His tongue ran fleetingly over my bottom lip, as if tasting me.

"Ah, Miel," he whispered with a sigh.

His lips found mine again, and the world slipped away as it had when he'd taken my hand at the villa. We weren't an American who would soon leave and a Beaumontian who would stay. There was no sister to find, or other place to go. We were simply two people absorbed by an incredibly strong attraction.

"Miel," he whispered again, finally releasing my lips. His eyes were molten gold, searing me with his stare before he pulled me to his chest.

"We'd probably better get back to the others," I said.

He grinned reluctantly. "My mother will be waiting with lunch."

Ah, yes, the mother. I was even more nervous to meet her now that he'd kissed me. He leaned over for one more slow kiss that sent spirals of heat into my belly. Then he took my hand and we started back.

"So," I said as casually as I could, "I guess you take all your dates here."

He stopped walking and looked at me, a smile on his face, his eyes dancing. "Then you admit this is a date."

The most wonderfully exciting date of my life, which I wasn't going to admit because it would show how pathetic I really was. "If you insist."

"Ah, Miel," he said, his face sobering in that sudden way of his, "you are the only girl I have ever brought here."

I believed him. "What does *miel* mean?" I asked, feeling a blush come to my cheeks.

"It means honey." It was his turn to look embarrassed. "It's just what I thought of when I first heard your name, and now that I have kissed you . . . Miel fits perfectly."

What could I say to that?

No wonder my sister had fallen in love with a Beaumontian. I might be doing the same thing.

$\mathcal{T}$he cottage was like something out of a fairy tale, making our cute villa look like the tourist trap it was. I'd thought it might be more like a cabin in the forest, but the moniker cottage fit it perfectly, though it was much larger than I'd imagined. It had a steeply gabled roof covered with what looked like terracotta shingles that had once been red but were now quaintly spotted with green and black moss. Copper trimmed the windows and the door, the pieces beautifully colored with water and age.

Damien's mother opened the door before we reached it. She looked a lot like Stéphanie but with short hair, and her eyes were lighter brown, more like Damien's golden color. She hugged her children tightly, and then hugged each of us too. "Welcome, welcome," she said in English that was every bit as good as her children's but accented differently. Damien had told me she'd lived a lot of her youth in Germany, so maybe that was it. "Please, call me Lucida. And come in. I'm sure you're hungry after the long drive."

I wasn't a bit hungry. In fact, the grounds surrounding the cottage beckoned for exploration. Tall trees grew next to the cottage, and rose bushes just beginning to bud lay in luscious flowerbeds that bordered the cobbled walk. The landscape was beautiful and well kept. Either Damien's mother employed a gardener or the family was serious about their yard work.

"Like it?" Lucida asked me.

"It's beautiful. And peaceful." I almost expected twelve dwarves to come out of the house, followed by a singing Snow White. I felt envious of Damien for growing up here.

"Damien will show you around after lunch. Come on." To my surprise, she put her arm around me and led me inside. I glanced behind me to find Damien grinning, and heat washed through me. Behind him, Harper and Emerson, each carrying a single backpack, were deep in a conversation about horses with Stéphanie. Emerson wore a smitten expression on his face that I recognized from the ten crushes he'd had during junior year before our homework load became too heavy for anything but study.

Inside, the cottage was open and simply decorated. "Your rooms are upstairs," Lucida said. "But we'll show you those later. Lunch is ready on the patio."

She led us to a small cobbled area in the back of the cottage. Trellises lay against the side of the house, where roses climbed in riotous abandon. Bushes and flowers and plants filled the flowerbeds even more abundantly than in the front. I loved it.

"I'm in the middle of putting this all to rights," Lucida said, waving toward an old wooden chair topped by garden shears and a hat.

"You do all this yourself?" Harper asked.

"Not the front. Just here." Lucida's grin reminded me of Damien's. "I like it a little wild."

We all agreed that it was perfect and sat down at the small table that was a little tight for six. We ate grilled chicken, vegetables, and some kind of pudding I didn't recognize. I was sure it was all wonderful, but I couldn't taste a thing. I was too busy noticing Damien's leg pressing against mine and his eyes that never seemed to leave my face. Every time he looked away, it was my turn to drink him in.

This couldn't be happening.

But it was.

Lucida kept the conversation rolling, as if she had long practice at it, and I was grateful. After we'd finished eating, I tried to clear the table, but her hand fell over mine. "You can help another time. Go let Damien show you around. The horses will be here soon." She glanced down at my bare legs. "But you might want to change into long pants."

Stéphanie showed Harper and me to a room on the cottage's second floor, where the ceiling slanted with the roof. There were two single beds, but to get to them, we had to stoop slightly to protect our heads.

"I keep expecting to see dwarves and Snow White," Harper said after Stéphanie left for her own room.

I laughed. "I know, right?"

Harper's smile vanished. "But this place . . . Mel, some of these decorations are expensive, and the paintings. I think Damien's family has money."

She'd graduated at the top of her design class, so she should know. An undefined disquiet crawled through me, though I couldn't say why it mattered. "Well, what's wrong with that? But maybe they've been in the family for a while. With all the discoloring of the roof and the patina on the copper, this place is definitely older then we are."

"You're probably right." She threw her backpack on one of the beds.

By the time we made it back outside the cottage, Stéphanie and Emerson were already there. They barely looked at us when we approached, and I felt an unfamiliar twinge of jealousy before I shrugged it off. I wanted Emerson to find the right woman. I just didn't want him to find her here. I didn't want to lose my friend when this whole Beaumontian thing was over.

All my thoughts fled as Damien came around a huge flowering bush, riding a horse and leading four more. I'd only ridden a couple times with Harper at her grandfather's house, and I hoped that would be enough to keep me from looking like an idiot.

I swung up onto one of the horses, and Damien smiled at me. That was good. The mare was beautiful and calm, and I soon lost myself in the rocking motion, the smell of spring, and Damien's smile.

We rode for thirty minutes, and then Damien motioned me over to a huge tree with branches that looked perfect for a treehouse. Sure enough, as we grew closer, I could see the green-painted wood someone had used to build one.

"Is it yours?" I asked with a laugh.

"You know it."

We dismounted and raced each other to climb the tree. Inside the little house, leaves littered the uneven floor, and the creaking was enough to make us both a little nervous.

"Haven't been here for a while," he said.

"A long while, I'm guessing."

Instead of going inside, I crawled out on a thick branch, and he followed me, straddling the branch. After a moment, he leaned forward and kissed me. My head whirled—not a good thing this far up, but I didn't care. I loved how his lips felt against mine. It was so . . . right.

I never wanted it to end.

But I knew it would have to eventually.

Damien

The day had been perfect. Stéphanie was right about coming here. Everything seemed frozen in time, and I didn't want it to end. I knew Monday would bring all kinds of reality to my life, but for now I was falling, falling, and for once I wasn't scared. Miel was real. I loved the way she'd climbed the tree and showed no fear going out onto the branch. I loved how she'd kissed me back with as much emotion as I'd kissed her.

My mother even approved—I could tell by her smiles and the way she talked to Miel. She'd never talked to anyone I'd dated like that, and certainly not to Bridgit or even Léandre, who'd visited our estate dozens of times. Maybe it was the cottage and the magic it had always held for my parents, but I thought it was Miel. I wondered if I could convince her not to leave.

I lay there for an hour, listening to Emerson's snores before I finally went downstairs. I wasn't hungry, but maybe a brisk walk would get my thoughts to shut down enough to sleep. I'd barely made it out of the room when I caught a glimpse of a figure going down the stairs.

"Miel?" I called, hurrying after her.

She turned as she reached the bottom and looked up at me. Her thick hair was in complete disarray, and her tank top and sleeping shorts were twisted slightly. Her half-lidded eyes and translucent skin spoke of sleep, but the terror lurking in her face told me something was wrong.

"What is it?" I hoped she wasn't being bothered by the spiders that sometimes infested that room.

"I—uh." Tears started, and in the next minute I was down the stairs, holding her in my arms.

"What happened?"

Her chest heaved. "Nothing. Just . . . a bad dream."

A *really* bad dream by the look of it. "Come on. Let's sit on the sofa."

She clung to me as I led her there. I turned on the table lamp and sat next to her, pulling her close and covering her with one of my mother's afghans.

"Do you want to tell me about it?"

She shook her head.

"I can make us some hot chocolate."

"No, please. Just . . . don't leave."

The request tore something inside me. This wasn't the Miel I'd come to know these past couple days, and it bothered me that she appeared so haunted. This didn't seem to be a one-time incident.

She turned in my arms, and I could tell she wanted to kiss me. I held her tighter, telling myself that under no circumstances was I going to allow myself to kiss her when she was so fragile.

"Oh, I have an idea." I popped up from the couch. "I brought you something. Should be around here. I only took up one of my bags."

There, in the corner. I fumbled through the larger suitcase, bringing out the 3D puzzle where I'd stashed it. "Look, it's a puzzle. Since you're so good at building things, I thought you'd like it. You know, being an engineer and all."

A smile worked through her fear. "It's *so* not the same thing. You know that, right?"

"Yeah, yeah. But don't tell me you never put one together before."

She shook her head. "Not one of these. We built plenty of our own with toothpicks or paper, though, for school." She shook her head. "Thanks. I'd love to build this with you."

I wasn't about to tell her that I'd bought it for her to take home, because doing it together was a thousand times better. I opened the box and shook the pieces out onto the coffee table. Within minutes we were hard at work, gluing piece after piece. She seemed to know instinctively what went next, while I had to examine the instructions. Finally, I satisfied myself by swabbing glue on the pieces and watching her work, her wild hair tucked behind her ears and her teeth gnawing her lip.

She was so beautiful.

The next minute she looked up at me, catching my stare. Dropping the pieces of paper, she hugged me. "Thank you," she whispered.

"I don't know what you dreamed, but I wish I could help."

She pulled back slightly, meeting my eyes. "You have."

Her gaze fell, her lashes leaving shadows on her cheeks, and I could tell there was more. I held my breath so I wouldn't spoil the moment.

"I told you I only met my dad once," she said, "and that was true, but there was another man that I thought for my whole life was my father. And he wasn't the best father, but I loved him and he was mine, or so I thought. But when my mom died, he didn't even wait for the funeral to take me to my grandmother. I'd never met her, and she smelled funny. She was scary to me. When I begged him to stay, he told me he wasn't my father. Then he turned around and left, and I never saw him again. For a long time, it felt as if both my parents had abandoned me. When you're six, that's what death is like. Sometimes, I dream about that day when he left me."

I should have known it was something far worse than spiders. I slid my arms around her. "I'm sorry."

The words were inadequate, but she smiled and leaned into me. "It's really okay. The funny thing is that when I finally got over the shock of him leaving like that, I was glad. I used to dream about my real father coming to find me. And then he did."

The way she said it was casual, but I knew from the restaurant it didn't end well. "He died."

She nodded. "I was seven, and he came to see me for Christmas. Brought me a Cabbage Patch doll called Galinda Rosemary." Her smile deepened with the memory. "She had yellow yarn hair, bright blue eyes, and a pink gingham dress. It was seriously the best present I'd ever received, especially after moving to my grandmother's. I'd take the doll out only once a week to play with—I still have the box and she looks perfectly new. Anyway, my father had been in prison because of drugs—he'd been a crystal meth addict. But he was out, and he told me things were going to be different. That he had some things to work out with his family, and then he'd come back for me. But he never did because he was killed in a car accident."

She looked up, still sad but in control. "The worst thing about it wasn't losing him, because I didn't know him, but losing the dream, you know? There was no one else that could come for me. I was stuck with my grandmother, who was . . . well, let's just say emotionally distant."

I held her close, wishing I could take it away. I'd lived such a pampered life by comparison. Even when my father died, I'd had my mother and Stéphanie. Not to mention both grandmothers . . . and Léandre. No wonder it had taken me so long to grow up, to take over the estate and inherit my father's legacy. With all the support, I hadn't really needed to.

"It wasn't all bad," Miel added, as if sensing my compassion. "My grandmother taught me self-reliance. Good old grandmother."

She turned to face me. "I feel a lot better. You're a good listener."

I kissed her then because she was strong again. When we came up for air, I reluctantly let her go back to building the puzzle. She already had the main section of the royal palace halfway built. "These are fun," she said. "Thank you. I think I'll start a collection, though getting this one home might be a problem.

I laughed. "Guess you'll have to stay here."

We locked eyes, and there was that breathless feeling again that I always seemed to have around her. I fumbled for something to say. "So why did you choose to visit Beaumont? Was it really all the media attention?" Because now that I knew her better, she didn't seem the type to give much heed to that sort of thing.

If I hadn't been watching her so closely, I wouldn't have seen the sudden trembling of her hand. "Maybe," she said, "I came to meet you."

It wasn't an answer, and I had the distinct feeling she was hiding something, but I had two and a half months before she went back to America. Maybe by then we'd both spill our secrets.

*T*he next morning, I took them on a tour of our oldest factory, first alerting the management not to address me by my title. This was accomplished only by the manager going ahead of us to each area to warn the workers, most of whom I knew by name. Some I'd known as a young child. I didn't mind the curious stares and the winks behind Miel's back, but guilt assaulted me. I'd tell her the truth tonight, or the minute we were alone.

We started the tour by tasting the fresh olives and ended by sampling the different oils with bread. Then I gave them each a bottle to take home. "I'd seriously get fat if I lived here," Harper said. "As it is, I'm going to have trouble fitting into my wedding dress."

Miel laughed. "Graham will love you anyway."

"I don't know about that."

"Olive oil isn't fattening," Stéphanie said. "At least that's what we're sticking to. How about going riding again? After all this food, we can skip lunch and take a picnic for afternoon tea."

Everyone was excited about the idea, so I dropped them back at the cottage to change while I headed over to my estate for the horses. As I turned onto the road leading to the manor, I thought about what else I could do with Miel and her friends. Tomorrow was Saturday, the day of the charity ball, and I wondered if there was any chance she'd agree to go with me.

My stableboy had the horses ready when I arrived, but my stomach lurched when I saw he wasn't alone. Léandre and Bridgit were also there, dressed for riding.

"I thought you weren't coming," I said, wishing they hadn't.

"We changed our mind, and your butler—Enzo, isn't it?— was kind enough to put us up here last night. When we heard you were going riding, we decided to tag along with your new friends."

Bridgit smiled as she lifted her cheek to receive my perfunctory kiss. "We wanted to make sure you weren't being taken advantage of, darling. Will you help me up?"

I lifted her into the saddle, not knowing why I was so disgruntled to see them. Though we hadn't been together very much this past year, I owed Léandre a lot from the years we'd been close. "Well, you start out, and take the other horses. I'm just going to change my clothes."

"What if we get lost?" Bridgit asked.

Léandre rolled his eyes. "You must be joking. I've been riding here as often as on my own estate."

Probably more, if I were to estimate. Léandre didn't spend much time at home.

Fifteen minutes later, I caught up to them just before they reached the cottage. I reined in my horse from his gallop, and he slowed after I urged him to take the lead.

At the cottage, the others were waiting outside for us. When I saw Miel, my worry vanished. Her jeans and thin white sweater did amazing things to her figure, and best of all was the smile she gave me. Yet her expression faltered when she saw Léandre and Bridgit behind me. I wished I had somehow managed to lose them.

"Who's the other babe?" Léandre said under his breath as he looked at Harper.

"She's engaged," I said.

"Who cares?"

Stifling a groan, I moved past him. Unless I could somehow get rid of him, this was going to be a long ride.

Amelia

Stéphanie must have heard my exclamation of dismay when Damien returned not only with the horses, but with his friends from the lodge in tow. "Oh, Léandre's not all that bad," Stéphanie said. "I know he comes across like a jerk, but he's okay once you know how to take him. He's been a loyal friend to Damien, and sometimes he's a lot of fun."

Emerson made a noise in his throat. "He rides like he thinks he's a prince, or something."

Stéphanie choked on the soda she was drinking. "Well, he came into a big estate very young, but he doesn't have much to do with running it. I think that's part of his problem. He has a lot of growing up to do."

"Sounds like too much money and too much time," Harper murmured, and I nodded in agreement. People could say what they wanted about my grandmother's stinginess, but at least she'd forced me to take responsibility.

"His mother has control of his funds," Stéphanie added. "If she cut him off, maybe he'd change. Look, let's talk about it later. I don't want Damien to hear us. He knows Léandre has problems, but they go way back."

Damien came to a stop and dismounted. "Look who I ran into." His smile didn't reach his eyes, and I felt better knowing he wasn't happy about the intrusion either. He made the introductions quickly before asking me, "Can I help you up?"

I didn't need help, but I wasn't going to turn him down, not with that pipsqueak staring at him with her vulture eyes. "Your mother lent me some old boots because I left my shoes near the back door last night and the sprinklers got them."

He grimaced as he glanced down. "She lent you those old things?"

"Come on. They're perfect. And very comfortable."

As if unable to resist, he leaned forward and gave me a quick kiss. Behind him, I caught a glimpse of Bridgit glaring at me. *Okay.* That was one girl I wasn't going to win over.

After boosting me onto my horse, Damien went to help Stéphanie tuck our lunches into their saddlebags. They ended up going inside for additional food because of Léandre and Bridgit, so while we waited for them, Harper moved her horse closer to mine.

"Mmm, that kiss . . . looks like things are going well between you and Damien. I saw the palace you two were building last night. You must have been up for hours."

"I do like him—a lot," I admitted. "I never imagined when we came here that I'd meet someone like Damien. It seems like I've known him for months, but it's only been, what, four days—and you can't really count our first meeting."

Harper smirked. "He was half naked. We can definitely count it. The question is, how does he make you feel?"

"Well, sometimes it's as comfortable as being with Emerson, but"—I heaved sigh—"there's so much more to it."

Like how I could drown in his kisses and never come up for air. Like how I wanted to forget my upcoming job or going back to America. "At the same time, it feels like he's hiding something, you know?"

"Well, if he is, his mother and sister are in on it." Harper studied me for a moment. "When you think about it, we all hide things. You haven't told him everything."

My horse shifted under me, and I leaned forward and patted her neck. "I told him about my mom dying and Jud leaving me with my grandmother. And how I hoped my real dad would come for me and about the present he gave me."

Harper's eyes opened wide. "All that?"

"Last night. Scary, huh?"

She nodded. "No wonder you're freaked. You don't tell anyone that stuff. But you didn't tell him about Kami Fairbanks being your sister, did you?"

"No. It was already emotional enough, and there wasn't any way to pop it into the conversation—oh, and by the way, your queen is my half sister."

"Sounds a little crazy."

"Exactly. Anyway, if things don't work out with Kami, I'd rather leave it for later when it's not so fresh. Besides, there's nothing he can do about it. It's not like he can just give her a call and introduce me."

"No, but maybe these snotty friends of his can." She drew out her phone. "The name's Léandre Duvauchelle, right? That name is familiar, so I've probably run across it before. I'll do a search. Even if Léandre doesn't have an invitation to that ball tomorrow night, maybe he knows someone who does." She drew out her phone as

Damien finished with the food and climbed back onto his horse, urging it in our direction.

Damien watched with a smile as Harper rode off after the others, her phone in her hand. "Only Harper could text as she rides," he said.

I laughed, loving the feel of his leg as it brushed against mine.

We had barely started off when Harper waved for my attention, holding her phone up briefly before shoving it into her pocket. She'd found something, but whatever it was would have to wait.

We followed a small, gurgling river for about forty minutes, talking and laughing. Suddenly, Damien muttered something in French that sounded like a curse and spurred his horse toward the front of our caravan, where Léandre was in the lead. I was surprised because whatever Léandre's purpose, it hadn't seemed to be directed at torturing anyone, for which I was grateful. But while he and Damien were occupied, maybe I could ask Harper what she'd learned.

Seconds later, all thoughts of catching up with Harper fled as we came upon the most idyllic scene I'd ever witnessed. Beyond a small field of tiny purple flowers, the river had widened and water nearly spilled over the short, pebble-lined bank. On the other side of the river, a group of trees grew together, arching up and curving over like some sort of cave. The ground beneath this tree cave looked green with soft mosses and grass, a sharp contrast to the rocky bank.

Even Bridgit gasped with delight at the tree cave. She reigned her horse in and dismounted. "Oh, this little field is so beautiful. And those trees. Let's picnic there." It did seem perfect, and the water didn't look deep, so I bet we could cross.

"Don't, Bridgit," warned Damien. "It's not safe. We can get to the river and the trees by going around. Léandre shouldn't have led us this way."

"But the trees are right there through this small field." Bridgit took a step forward, looking like a miniature model in her pale tan riding breeches and her white blouse. "I don't want to go around. The horses will make it through the water just fine."

"Please, Bridgit," Damien said.

Bridgit gave him a little pout with her reddened lips. "Won't you come with me?" She raised her eyebrows and held out her hands in invitation. When Damien shook his head, she turned with a dramatic flair and started forward without him.

"Come back!" Stéphanie called. "He's not joking. It's not safe." But a hint of laughter seasoned her voice.

"Oh, let her go," Léandre said. "Maybe Mel and Harper want to go with her. It's very beautiful."

"No." Damien gave him a stern glance.

Bridgit walked farther into the field. "I'm not scared of snakes. That's what boots are for." As soon as the words left her mouth, she slipped and almost fell. "Bit muddy here."

"Because it's a mud pit!" Damien said. "It's *all* mud. Especially after the rains last week."

"Nonsense. I live in England. You Beaumontians have no idea what rain is." She slipped again and practically skated a few steps forward. She was halfway through the field now.

Damien blew out a frustrated breath. "Can't you see the banks have spilled over here?" He turned to Léandre and growled. "This is your fault. You're going after her."

"She's a big girl," Léandre replied. "Well, she's not big, of course, but she's old enough to decide for herself."

"You should have warned her." Damien glanced at me and back at Léandre.

"Come on, you guys, it's—" Bridgit gave a scream as she suddenly fell backwards onto her bottom. She scrambled up, only to fall again on her knees. "Help! It's sucking at me!" She stood and fell again.

Léandre and Emerson laughed, and even Stéphanie wore a smile. Bridgit was quickly becoming covered in mud, and she did look ridiculous. Every time she stood and took a step, her shiny boots skidded out from under her and dumped her back into the mud.

"You knew this would happen!" she shouted at Léandre, who was off his horse now and doubling over with laughter. Finally, Bridgit remained sitting in the mud, tears leaking down her cheeks.

"Oh, for crying out loud." I slid off my horse and started across the field, following Bridgit's trail of trampled flowers. After a few steps, the mud slurped at my boots.

"No, I'll go!" Damien dismounted quickly and started after me.

He was too late. I reached Bridgit without falling and gave her a hand up. "Thanks," she said with a wet hiccup.

I put an arm around her, and we took a step forward. I was silently congratulating myself when my feet slid suddenly to the side. We both tumbled into the mud, squishing more flowers into oblivion. Damien reached us, and we made it a couple more steps before we all fell again in a tangled heap.

"There's really no way out but to crawl," he said, staying where he'd fallen next to me. "This is the slipperiest mud in all the world. We have no idea why. But it is." Taking his finger, he touched my cheek, drawing something with mud. It felt like a heart. "Did anyone ever tell you that you look great in mud?"

"No, but so do you." I picked up a handful and smeared it on his head.

"Oh, yeah?" He lunged at me, pushing me backward into the sloppy mess. Bridgit screamed again as mud splashed onto her hair. To my surprise, Léandre headed into the field toward Bridgit. He didn't make it all the way before he fell flat on his face. I liked him better for it.

Emerson came next, followed by Stéphanie, and soon we were all slipping and slinging mud at each other and laughing—except Harper who just watched. The flowers had all disappeared by the time we crawled over to the river and fell inside the water. "Your mother's going to kill me for ruining her boots," I told Damien as I poured water from them.

"Are you kidding?" He laughed, dumping out his own boots. "This isn't the first time they've been in that field. They'll be fine—they just have to be dried out right. She'll take care of them."

By the time we were semi clean, Harper had found a way around with all the horses, and we picnicked under the tree cave next to the river. "You brought me here on purpose," Bridgit accused Léandre, her fork spearing a thin slice of roast. In my opinion, she looked much improved without her hair spray and so much makeup.

Léandre lifted his dark head from the mossy ground. "Yeah, but if you knew how sexy you looked in mud, you wouldn't mind."

Bridgit's mouth closed, and she stared at him as if she'd never seen him before. Then she recovered, and her gaze drifted to where I lay on the moss. "Thank you for coming after me. That was nice." It was probably the closest I'd get to an apology from the girl, and I was fine with that. I had to admit that I was impressed she hadn't made more of a fuss. I only hoped that didn't mean she had her claws out for Damien.

My attention was diverted as Damien rolled closer and put his arms around me. I snuggled against him. "Hey, when we get back, you want to go on a walk alone?" he whispered. "There's something I want to show you."

The way he said it told me it was important. Maybe I could tell him my secrets too.

$\mathcal{M}$y white sweater was never going to be the same, but I would keep it forever to remember this day. Thankfully, Damien's mother wasn't upset over the boots, and she took them from me with a laugh. "They'll be good as new when Margaux gets them." She laughed. "Or rather, as good as they were before today."

I didn't know who Margaux was, but it wasn't my place to ask. "Thanks for the loan."

"That mud field is treacherous, but I can't bear to have it filled in. I met Damien's father there. I'll tell you the story sometime."

I was flattered that she thought I'd be around long enough.

"Come on, Mel." Harper grabbed my arm. "You should shower and change while Damien returns the horses."

Damien looked ready to object, but Bridgit grabbed his arm. "Please, let's take them back. My stuff's all there, and I need to get out of these clothes."

That started Léandre laughing again, and Damien met my eyes with a little shrug as Harper waved goodbye and pulled me inside and up the stairs to our room. Emerson followed us up.

"I think he was going to show me something," I said to my friends.

Emerson grunted. "Not with those two around."

"Well, they aren't as bad as they were the first time I met them."

"They're bad enough, but at least Damien picks you over them, every time." Harper pulled out her phone. "Still, we may need

Léandre. Or should I call him His Lordship? Léandre Duvauchelle is the Baron de Accolay."

"Baron?" I gasped.

"Yes. I knew I'd seen him somewhere. He was in an article written in England, but there are a ton of other articles. I only had time to look at the first couple."

Emerson grabbed the phone and peered at the screen. "Huh, what do you know? This was written two weeks ago, and this other one was three weeks. Busy boy."

I had to see for myself. "No wonder he's so obnoxious." Worry slid over me, and for the first time since the mud field I thought about my sister. She was a queen, which was higher than a baron. I hoped that didn't mean she was as insufferable as Léandre.

"Well, it's not as high as a count or a prince, but he should have the connections you need." Harper leaned closer to me to catch my eyes. When I looked up from her phone, she continued, "You have to ask Damien to ask Léandre to get us in to the ball tomorrow night."

I shoved the phone at her. "How? What would I say?"

"That you're curious. You'd like to see the queen."

"What about the truth?" Emerson suggested.

Harper rounded on him. "No! He'll think she's nuts. Everyone knows the queen has no siblings. All Mel has is her grandmother's letter, and the doll he mentions."

"And the pictures." My grandmother had let him take us out to eat, and the place had a booth were we'd taken our picture. He'd kept two and so had I. I didn't know how to go about getting a DNA test, but I was sure Kami would want one done.

I walked across the room through the middle, avoiding the low parts of the ceiling. "Maybe I'll play it by ear?"

Harper nodded. "It's only natural you'd be curious about royalty since we don't have any in America."

I sighed. "It's all so complicated. I wish . . ."

That I didn't have a sister at all? That I didn't feel like a needy idiot for chasing a dream halfway around the world? Maybe it would be okay just to see her and get a feel for who she was. Then I could go home and write that letter Emerson kept urging me to write. I could tell her I didn't need or want her money, and after that, she could make the choice.

Arg! I let my head drop to my hands—and smelled something awful. "Ugh. I don't know what was in that mud, but I need a shower."

Damien would be back soon, and then I'd talk to him about the ball.

Damien

I held Miel's hand as we walked along a peaceful trail near the cottage. She'd been quiet during the dinner that my mother had somehow pulled off without her lady's maid or our cook. I wasn't sure why, but her silence worried me.

"Penny for your thoughts," I said to Miel.

She laughed softly. "I told you they were worth way more than that."

"Well, I meant a Beaumontian penny of course. They're worth more. Or were before euros."

"I hear everything was better before euros."

My turn to laugh. "Well, that's true." We walked a few more steps. Darkness was falling fast, and if I wanted to take her to my estate, I should do it sooner rather than later. I'd meant for her to come with me to return the horses, but with Léandre and Bridgit there, it was just as well Harper had pulled her away. "Is something wrong?"

Miel stopped walking. "Actually, yes." She grimaced, her nose wrinkling in a way that reminded me of the mud field and how she'd looked on the riverbank with her wet shirt clinging to every curve and tendrils of sopping hair cascading past her shoulders.

She's it. She's really it. The thought both thrilled and terrified me. "What?"

"Harper found out about Léandre. Why didn't you tell us he's a baron? I mean, that's something big around here, isn't it?"

"Well . . . uh, yes. But we've been friends a long time. I don't think of him that way." Was there more she wasn't saying? I hoped not; I didn't want her to find out about me from anyone else.

"Right, of course." She took a deep breath and plunged on. "Look, there's a charity ball tomorrow night. I know you and your sister have plans, but do you think Léandre . . . would he have tickets or any pull to get us in? Harper and me at least."

Something cold shuddered through my chest. My fingers let go of hers, and I folded my arms to cover my surprise. "You'd want to go to one of those?" I'd been thinking of asking her this morning, but having her bring it up threw me off—especially with Léandre involved.

Miel's gaze dropped. "Never mind. It's not important."

I grabbed her hand again as she started to walk away. "Wait. Tell me."

"It's nothing." Her lowered lashes made me think of last night when she'd told me about her father. There was more to her request—I could feel it.

Something stubborn in me pressed on. "It's just that I hadn't pictured you as one of those tourists who are always trying to catch a glimpse of the royal family." Or as someone who would use Léandre's position as a baron for her benefit, but I didn't say that aloud.

She bristled at my tone, and even I had to admit it was slightly accusatory. "Why wouldn't I want to go? I've never been to a ball before, and it's not like I'll ever get the chance again. In a couple months I'll be back in America. I just thought—it's at the palace. What other chance will I have to see it?"

I wanted to tell her she had every chance, and that she didn't ever have to leave Beaumont. That I could take her to meet Gabriel and Kami whenever she wanted. Another part of me felt hurt that she'd go with Léandre. Maybe she *was* looking for her prince.

Or baron.

Maybe she'd been at the Suite Royale with the idea to meet nobility. After all, that was where Gabriel had first met Kami. The idea made me angry.

"I was just curious, that's all." But I knew her well enough to recognize the tension in her face. What was she hiding? It had been real between us, hadn't it? She wasn't a married baroness or a stripper posing as a Spanish contessa.

The truth was, I really didn't know.

"I'm sure Léandre can get you in," I told her. "He'd be glad to. Harper and Emerson too." My own invitation would cover them all, but she didn't have to know that.

Because I didn't tell her.

"Oh, thank you!" Her cheeks flushed and her eyes brightened. "Look, I know it's a dinner and it's costly, but I have the funds. Tell him I'll pay the price of the tickets."

She had no idea how much they cost, especially purchased this late. She could buy plane tickets back to America for the cost—it was a fundraiser, after all. No way would I allow her to pay. "I'll talk to him."

She hugged me before turning around and starting down the path. "I'd better tell Harper. She'll be so excited."

I followed more slowly, a numbness settling over my heart.

"*S*he wanted nothing to do with Léandre," I told Stéphanie later that night. "She barely talked to him all day. But now she wants him to get her an invitation to the Children's Charity Ball. What am I supposed to think about that?"

Miel and her friends had already retired to their rooms, the girls talking about shopping in the morning. Ever since they'd left, I'd been venting in the kitchen to my sister. I didn't worry about them overhearing because they were up in the farthermost room, and even if they came down, we were speaking French far too quickly for them to understand.

"So? Léandre's a sarcastic jerk. I avoid him too." Stéphanie poured a cup of hot chocolate from the pan where she'd put fresh milk and pieces of gourmet Beaumontian chocolate. "As for the ball, Mel is visiting. They don't have royalty in America. She's probably just curious."

"I guess so. But it seemed more than that. Like she was . . . desperate to go." I shook the image from my head.

"It's not like she's going there to find a prince or anything." Stéphanie sat in the chair next to me, studying my face. "Wait. Really? That's what you're thinking?"

I scowled. "Well, there's good old Léandre, a rich baron. You saw how he was to her today—almost nice. He thinks she's hot, and maybe she was avoiding him because she actually likes him. You girls seem to do that sort of thing."

Stéphanie gawked at me, a grin coming to her face. "I can't believe you're jealous. Of Léandre! Even I know Mel better than to think she'd go after him. I think you're just upset because she's going to think it's Léandre giving her what she wants, and not you."

I had to admit there might be the tiniest bit of truth to that. "The really stupid thing is that I was thinking of telling her tonight. You know, taking her over to the estate and coming clean. I was even thinking of inviting her to the ball myself."

Stéphanie leaned over and bumped my shoulder with hers. "Then I was right. The real reason you're upset is that Léandre will be her hero. You're jealous, plain and simple."

"Well, if we take them to the ball, I'll have to tell her." Fierce satisfaction filled me at that because she'd know she had me to thank.

"I could still play interference. You know, ward off anyone who wants to talk business while you're with her."

"No." I shook my head. "It's gone far enough." I stared down at my untouched chocolate. "I think I'm falling for her—and hard. It isn't fair not to tell her. Letting her find out from someone else might ruin everything. Like it or not, my title and our money is a part of me."

Or was I telling myself this because I was afraid I'd lose her to some noble playboy? I mean, I didn't really know her, did I? Maybe that's what she was looking for, and I was a simple distraction.

Stéphanie watched me with a knowing smile. "Even if it means she might want you for your money? I mean, she did grow up pretty poor, from what I gather. Harper tells me she cleaned houses all through college."

Something in me rankled at that. Not because she'd cleaned houses or worked as a maid, but because Miel was so much more than that. "She's not a poor little girl anymore. She's a fighter. She's educated. She has a good job lined up. Mother even likes her. I just wish I knew why the ball is so important to her." I swirled the milk in the mug and some sloshed over the side. I couldn't drink it if I tried. "Stéphi, what if in two months she still leaves me and goes back to America?"

"I don't know." Stéphanie sipped her chocolate. "Maybe you should go ask her."

"I can't. They said something about getting an early start. Shopping or something."

Stéphanie blinked at me for a few silent moments, and then a gasp escaped her throat. "The ball. Oh, no! They won't have the right clothes—or *any* appropriate clothes."

"She doesn't need a famous designer dress like at the Autumn Debutante Ball," I said. "And she'll look great in anything." *Even mud.* In fact, I wished we were going back to that field tomorrow instead of to the charity ball.

"No, no, no." Stéphanie stood. "Think of how women like Bridgit will treat her—especially if they believe she's stealing one of *their* eligible bachelors."

"We'll go to a store and help them find something."

"Not going to happen. There won't be anything available this late—and all the designers already have their gowns being worn by anyone with a half-decent figure." She stood up, bumping the table and causing more of my chocolate milk to slosh over the rim. "We have to talk to Mom! She'll know what to do!"

We hurried to the far side of the cottage, where we found our mother in her bedroom, not only awake, but throwing a few things into a small suitcase. "Where are you going?" Stéphanie asked.

"I'm glad you're here, but I hope I didn't wake you." She looked fleetingly at us as she zipped the bag. "I just had a call from Enzo, and he says Teresa is throwing up. I need to go to her. You know how she gets. I've called Margaux back to fill in for her while she's down." Teresa was our ancient cook at the estate, and she was rarely sick, but when she was, she needed a lot of tender care.

Stéphanie sighed. "She's such a baby!"

"Stéphi!" Our mother frowned at her.

"Well, people throw up. It happens. She's old enough not to act like a baby about it."

"She's been with us so long; she's part of the family. I need to go to her." My mother reached for her suitcase, but I beat her to it. "Did you need something before I leave?" she asked.

I glanced at Stéphanie and shook my head slightly. I didn't want to add to my mother's trouble. I knew people, and I'd pull in some favors if that's what it took to help Miel.

"Damien, I saw that," said my mother. "What's going on?"

"Nothing we can't handle," he insisted. "You go take care of Teresa."

"We cannot handle it!" Stéphanie said. "Damien's gone and invited Mel and her friends to the ball tomorrow. They won't have anything to wear!"

"They're going shopping tomorrow," I protested. "I know a few people to call."

My mother's face paled. "No, Damien. That won't do. I'm not a snob by any means, but you are the Comte de Laval, and if you care about her, Amelia needs to be dressed properly. This is the biggest event in Beaumont this year. Everyone of importance will be there."

"I thought of lending her one of my dresses, but everyone will know it's mine—especially those hateful gossip columnists." Stéphanie sat down on the bed. "They seem to track everything I do when I'm in Beaumont. At least Damien can lend Emerson clothes. They'll only be a little too long."

Our mother thought a moment. "I know what to do. I have plenty of dresses no one has seen in a very long time, and fortunately, retro happens to be in."

"Yes! That should work," Stéphanie said with a little bounce.

"Remember when we were trying on our new dresses in your room, and I said it looked like some of your old ones? But what if they don't fit?"

"Oh, I was thinner then. About Amelia's size. Margaux will come back in the morning with a few for both girls to try on. She's good with a needle, and I think she can work something out. Now I'd better get to Teresa. I wish I could be there for you both tomorrow night, but it's unlikely I'll be able to leave her."

I walked her out to her car. "Mom," I began, after putting her suitcase in the trunk.

She reached up and laid her hand on my face. "I know, son. I can see it in your eyes. You like this girl, but you're worried because everything's not perfect. Well, let me tell you, it never is. It's working through the bumps that shows what you're made of."

"I should have told her who I was from the beginning."

"Yes, but I know why you didn't. Your father made me wait two years to prove I wasn't after his money. I hope it doesn't take that long to work this out." Her hand dropped from my cheek.

I watched her car recede from view, then turned in the driveway and looked up at the room above my mother's where I knew Miel probably lay sleeping.

I used to wonder what it would be like to care about someone enough to imagine a life with them, but these past few days when I closed my eyes, Miel was always there in any future I could conceive. It was like my father once told me about my mother: "That's how I knew she was the one. Every time I pictured my future, she was there beside me."

"I hope this is only a bump," I told Miel's window. "Because if it's something more, I don't know if I can get over you."

Amelia

I stared at myself in the full-length mirror Stéphanie had brought to our room from somewhere else in the house. I barely recognized myself. Harper had styled my hair and put on my makeup, and the red dress hugged all the right curves, the silk gently widening until the bottom swished around my heels and made me feel like a princess. Margaux—who turned out to be a friend of Damien's mother—had done a great job at taking in the waist so it fit perfectly.

Between the makeup and the bold color of the dress, my eyes appeared almost too large in my face. To top it all off, I wore the simple silver locket Emerson had given me for Christmas and the fake diamond studs I'd had since high school. There was also a shawl that was far too delicate to keep me warm, but it was beautiful.

"Where did you say your mom got these dresses?" Harper asked, equally mesmerized by the one she wore. Her dress had an empire waist and was a deep red that looked great with her dark hair.

"Oh, she saved them from when she was our age. I'm not sure where she wore them. Maybe a dance?" Stéphanie said. "Who knows?"

The statement didn't ring quite clear, but I was too excited to protest. I was going to meet Kami. Finally. Dressing up was fun, and having Damien go with me was a bonus, but meeting Kami was everything.

"Shall we go?" Harper asked. "It's an hour drive, right?"

"At least. But wait here. I need to get something." Stéphanie turned in a rustle of white silk and hurried out the door.

"Damien is going to eat you up in this," Harper said. "You look . . . well, like an heiress."

"I don't know. When I first asked him to talk to Léandre, it was like I'd punched him in the gut. You should have seen his expression."

Harper rolled her eyes. "He's worried you're into barons, is all."

"Maybe." I didn't think so, though. My request had completely changed him toward me. I hoped it would pass.

There was no time for further discussion because Stéphanie was already coming back inside the room. "Okay, Mel, I want you to wear this. I bought it just a few days ago, and I think it goes perfectly with your dress." She handed me a box, and I pulled out a sparkling tiara. "Oh, it's beautiful! But you should wear it."

"I have others I can wear." She hefted another larger box in her hand, opening it to reveal several more tiaras, each wrapped in tissues.

"Why do you have so many?" I asked.

She laughed. "I sort of collect them." She held the box out to Harper. "Go ahead, pick."

Harper squealed and reached for one with the tiniest red stones sprinkled among what had to be fake diamonds.

Stéphanie chose one with all diamonds, slightly thinner than the one I wore. "Come on," she said.

I brought up the rear as we glided down the stairs—or at least I tried to glide. The heels I'd borrowed were slightly too large, and I needed to tighten the straps.

The men waited in the hallway below, both dressed in tuxedos, and Damien drew in a sharp breath as he saw me. "*Que belle,*" he murmured. I smiled, thinking that he looked pretty good himself.

"You can say that again." Emerson's gaze went from me to Harper to Stéphanie. "Even I know what that means."

Damien had eyes only for me, but I was every bit as guilty for staring. He was so handsome and perfect. Yummy. I wanted to freeze this moment forever, when there was just us standing here drinking in each other.

Harper cleared her throat. "Uh, we don't want to be late."

I let Damien take my hand and lead me outside to a limousine with a driver. Years of frugality made me want to protest the luxury, but Harper had read to me about how everyone arrived in expensive cars with drivers. I'd have to remember to thank Léandre for his generosity.

Or had it been Damien? I'd hate for him to use his hard-earned money on my whims when I was perfectly able to pay for myself. I'd have to make it up to him.

The 3D puzzle didn't do justice to the majesty of the Beaumontian palace. The engineer part of me marveled at the arches and the towers and the height of the walls. Designing something like this would be an accomplishment of a lifetime. But the woman who'd been abandoned by her parents as a child felt overwhelmed at the luxury of the entryway. One thought kept recurring: Kami was a queen, and her husband had two sisters. She didn't need me.

We were slightly late, so the reception line had already disbanded and people were sitting down in the banquet hall. Scores of servants awaited to direct guests to their numbered tables, and armed guards ringed the room. Gilt decorations, statues, paintings, and mirrors—the visual stimulation was more than I was prepared to deal with. Thankfully, Damien was still holding my hand.

I could see Kami standing at a table clear across the room, too far from where we were being directed to allow me to address her. I couldn't simply break away and accost her. Disappointment flooded through me, and I fought to blink back tears. All this work, all this preparation, and I wasn't going to get within a hundred feet of her.

Unless maybe Léandre could introduce me?

Damien released my hand. "I'll meet you at the table, okay? It's at the end of this row." He indicated the line of round tables next to us.

I nodded, though I wanted to cling to him. Where was he going when I needed him? He seemed much more comfortable here than I felt.

I stood still, watching him stride in the direction of a man who stood some distance away. Before Damien reached him, another man intercepted Damien and the two began talking. It looked like business. Maybe someone Damien knew from the olive oil factory.

"Oh, there's Léandre," Harper said, waving. A few of the elegant people stared at her, and at least one camera flashed. The royal guards had made the general attendees check any cameras at the door with their shawls and purses, allowing only a few chosen media personnel to record the event. I bet at least one of them was watching Léandre to see if he did anything interesting upon meeting us.

Léandre met us halfway to the table, bending over to kiss our cheeks. "It took some doing," he said, "but we're all at the same table."

"Hello," Bridgit said coming out from behind him and startling me with the suddenness of her appearance.

"Hi," I said.

"Oh, you're wearing Stéphanie's new tiara. It's beautiful. And your dress is lovely." She seemed surprised, but I tried not to take offense. "Who's the designer? I'll have to give them some business."

I was rescued from answering her question when a young man strode up to our group. "Lady Rothschild," he said stiffly, "will you save me a dance tonight?"

Lady. So Bridgit was nobility, though like with Léandre, Damien hadn't introduced her as such.

Bridgit let him kiss her gloved hand. "Sure, Gianni," she said. Smiling, he dipped his head and walked quickly away.

"Really, him?" Léandre gazed at her with a little sneer.

"Come on. The queen has signaled the servers to begin dinner," Stéphanie said.

Bridgit linked arms with me as we hurried to the table. She was being positively nice, which confused me after her pointed stares the previous day. Maybe she was still feeling grateful that I'd tried to save her from the mud.

"You know," she said, "I was practically engaged to Gabriel once before *she* came along. She stole him right out from under me."

Next to her, Stéphanie rolled her eyes, making Emerson snort.

Ignoring them all, I stood next to our table and watched the queen make her way up to a raised dais. She was tall, dark-haired, and beautiful. So sure of herself.

So unlike me.

"Miel?" Damien appeared beside me, his hands on the back of my chair. "May I seat you?" Belatedly, I realized that Léandre and Emerson had already seated the other women—though where Emerson had learned such manners was beyond me.

"Yes, please."

What I really wanted was leave here and go riding with him. Maybe to the mud field. Even going back to the lodge and unclogging toilets sounded less upsetting.

Stifling a sigh, I sat and tried to enjoy myself. I only wished my heart would stop banging against my chest.

$\mathcal{D}$amien was charming during dinner and almost made me forget my worries about meeting Kami. He was casual about addressing the waiter assigned to our table and knew exactly which of the many forks to use.

He looks like he belongs here, I thought.

More so than Léandre, who was drinking too much and talking too loud. At least Léandre was still being nice to me, if overly attentive to Harper, who seemed to conveniently forget she was engaged. Every time she leaned over to talk to him, Bridgit glared at them both, which almost made me laugh out loud. Bridgit had to be bipolar if one minute she was eyeing Damien and the next jealous of Léandre's attention to Harper.

When the dancing began, Damien led me to the ballroom and out on the floor, where I found myself grateful for the semester of ballroom dance I'd squeezed in at Stanford. His cheek came to rest on mine, and all thoughts of Kami fled. I'd died and gone to heaven, having him this close. "I could get used to this," I murmured.

He stiffened and his face went blank. "So you like this life?"

Life? What was he talking about? He seemed to be making some point, but I was in too much turmoil to figure out what it was. Because in that instant all the peace I'd felt with him vanished and the worry about Kami came flooding back.

"It's very beautiful," I murmured. Or it might be if I wasn't getting an ulcer. The night was draining away. If I didn't find Léandre and get him to introduce me to Kami, I might never get up the courage again.

At that moment, I caught a glimpse of Kami across the room. My sister, Beaumont's new queen, was so much . . . more than I could ever be.

"What's wrong?" Damien asked.

"I'm feeling a little nauseated," I admitted. I didn't know what was worse, Damien's strange comment or the gnawing battle going on in my stomach.

Immediately, he was all concern, and with his arm around me, he led me off the dance floor. "There's a powder room, if you need one."

Now that he mentioned it, my bladder did feel close to bursting. "Where?"

"Out here." He led me past the guards near the door and out into the huge hallway. "It's just through there." He pointed to an open door. "Would you like me to get you a drink?"

That was better than having him wait outside the door. "Yes, thank you." I was grateful to be alone for a moment. I needed to decide what to do about Kami, but it was awfully hard with Damien acting so weird.

The bathroom had a grouping of plush couches for resting,

and a servant stood near a stack of cloth hand towels, and she handed one to each woman after she washed her hands. It didn't look like any bathroom I'd ever been in but rather like a beautiful sitting room that happened to have several connecting doors and a row of sinks.

Feeling only a tiny bit better, I left the bathroom and returned to the ballroom. Damien was nowhere in sight, but maybe I could find Léandre and get him to introduce me to Kami.

Wait. There was Kami now, not five paces from me, dancing with her husband. All I had to do was to go up and tap on her shoulder and ask to talk to her. I'd give her the copy of the letter I had slipped into my bra.

I began reaching for it, stepping forward quickly. What would I say? "Hi. You need to read this" didn't seem quite adequate, but neither did I want to make a scene by babbling on. I closed half of the space between us. She looked normal, and when she glanced briefly at me, she was smiling.

Okay, I can do this. Unexpected emotion rose up to form a lump in my throat. I still had family. Maybe.

The dance was drawing them away, but if I stepped a little closer, maybe I could find the courage to ask for a moment of her time.

My progress was abruptly halted when strong hands gripped my arms. I gave a little cry as I realized two of the royal guards held me in place, their fingers as strong as iron underneath their fastidious white gloves.

Kami and the king turned at the commotion, concern on their faces, but one of the guards bowed quickly and spoke in rapid French that I couldn't begin to understand.

Then I was dragged out of the ballroom. "What's going on?" I asked.

A light flashed in my eyes as someone snapped a picture. One of the guards peeled off me and went after the offender, so the snapshot was obviously not taken by an official photographer for the event. I could only imagine how many tabloids would have my face splattered across them in the morning.

"Where is the camera, miss?" The guard demanded the moment we'd cleared the door.

I gaped at him, wondering if I'd understood his heavily accented words correctly. "I don't have a camera!"

"You were reaching for something." His hand went to his very real sidearm.

I gulped noisily. This was going from worse to horrible. "I just wanted to talk to her. To show her this—" I went for the paper again.

"Stop!" He drew his weapon.

I lifted my hands in front of my face, all too aware of elegant people passing us and staring. Why had I ever come here? I wished I could melt into the floor and disappear.

Then Damien was at my side, pulling me to him and stepping between us. "She's with me. What's the problem here?"

The guard lowered his gun and saluted Damien. He rattled off something in French. I caught only the words "approaching the king."

"Speak in English," Damien told him.

The man bowed again, nearly dislodging his funny little hat. All his former confidence had disappeared. "She was reaching for something . . . in her . . . uh, dress." He motioned to his chest.

Damien looked over at me, his eyes grazing the place where my gown touched the swell of my breasts. More blood rushed to my face. "It wasn't anything! Just a piece of paper!" I drew it out with two fingers—slowly in case the guard went all Rambo on me again. Damien stared narrowly at the guard. "This is clearly a misunderstanding."

The guard nodded vigorously. "Yes, yes, Votre Seigneurie. I leave her to your care. But please keep her away from the king." He mumbled something else in French and marched off to the ballroom.

I shoved the note back into my bra. "Thanks."

Damien didn't smile. "What were you doing?"

Tears filled my eyes. "Like you said, it was a misunderstanding. But thanks for rescuing me."

The tension in his face eased. "Are you feeling better now? I'm afraid I no longer have your drink. I deposited it somewhere when I saw the guards leading you out."

Dragging me more like. "That's okay. I couldn't drink anything now anyway." It felt like we were strangers. For that alone, I wished I hadn't come tonight.

His touch was gentle as he eased me into his arms. Delicious goosebumps shuddered up my spine. "Let's forget this and go dance."

"All right."

I thought everyone might be staring at me as I entered the ballroom, but no one was. As Damien and I danced, I pondered my options. No way could I approach Kami now. I'd probably end up face-down on the floor with a gun pressed to my head. But maybe Léandre could help. My father's letter talked about both me and Kami. Maybe if he gave her the copy. Then she could find me if she was interested, and I wouldn't have to work at the lodge anymore. I could date Damien and spend time with my friends. I could stop obsessing about what I'd do if she rejected me.

I pulled away from Damien. "Can you excuse me? There's something I have to do."

"Give a note to the king?" There was an edge to the teasing in his voice.

"Look, I'll explain later. Right now, I have to talk to Léandre for a moment. It won't take long."

Damien studied me, a million questions in his eyes. I knew he wanted to know why. He probably thought I had a thing for barons. "It's not what you think."

"What do I think?"

When I didn't answer, he grabbed my hand and practically pulled me to where Léandre was dancing with Bridgit. He tapped on Léandre's shoulder. "Amelia would like to dance with you." He gave Bridgit an elegant bow. "If you will do me the honor of permitting me to be your partner."

She dipped her head with a smile. "Of course."

Damien dancing with Bridgit wasn't what I'd wanted at all, but it was too late. They moved off, with Bridgit snuggling way too close to him for my comfort.

"Was there something you wanted?" Léandre asked me, his gaze a bit mocking.

I dragged my gaze from Damien and Bridgit. "Oh, yes. Um." I tried to gather my thoughts as I focused on his eyes. He was rather handsome looking at me like that, but I didn't like how tightly he was gripping my waist. "Look, do you know the queen well enough to, uh . . . this might sound weird, but I need to give her something. It's really kind of . . . I think she'll want it, and if you'll just give it to her . . . well, this may be my only chance. It's important. Please." I hated asking him for anything, but he'd been nice yesterday and tonight. Completely different from the arrogant man I'd met at the lodge.

Léandre held me out at arms' length. "Why don't you ask Damien?" He lifted an arm and motioned for Damien and Bridgit to follow us as he led me off the dance floor to a quiet corner near one of the three entrances. The guards there watched me with suspicious eyes, and my stomach churned.

"Damien?" I asked. Léandre wasn't making sense. "But you're the one with the connections, the whole reason we were able to come tonight."

Léandre uttered something that resembled a snort more than it did a laugh. "Is that what you think? Didn't Damien tell you?" He shook his head. "Well, that's taking a wager a little too far."

Wager? Léandre was speaking English in that proper British accent of his, but it might as well be Cockney or some other British dialect that escaped my understanding.

"What is it?" Damien asked Léandre as he reached us, his voice untypically brusque.

"She needs to give Kami something. Why haven't you introduced them?"

Damien stared at me as if I'd betrayed him somehow. "I didn't know she wanted to meet Kami."

The tears were threatening again. This had gone so very wrong. "It's not like that."

"Then what is it?" That hard tone I didn't like was back in Damien's voice.

I fleetingly looked around for Harper and Emerson and caught sight of them on the dance floor. Harper glanced over at that moment. One glimpse of my face, and she grabbed Emerson's hand and started in my direction.

"There's something Kami needs to know," I said.

Léandre shrugged. "Well, Kami likes Damien far better than she does me. His Lordship actually shows up at the charity sponsor meetings, unlike certain others of us."

Charity sponsor meetings? His Lordship?

Then in a rush, it all made sense. Damien's importance at the factory, his ease at this ball, the way the guard had immediately deferred to him. It even explained his mother's dresses and Stéphanie's collection of tiaras.

"You're nobility?" I asked Damien. My heart thumped in protest.

Damien gave a sharp nod.

"He's the Comte de Laval," Bridgit said. "That's a count, in case you don't know."

I didn't take my eyes off Damien. With practiced effort, I held back my tears and instead stoked my fury. "You're the reason we're here tonight, and not Léandre? The horses are yours—and the factory? The land?" It was all so clear now. "Why didn't you tell me?"

"Why does it matter?" Damien's implication was clear. He thought I was after Léandre or even the queen because of the money. He hadn't wanted to tell me about his true life because I had no part in it—and never would. I was a money-grubbing commoner, good for a few laughs and kisses, and maybe, if he got lucky, a lot more.

"So this is just another game to you," I said between gritted teeth. *I will not cry in front of him. I will not!* "A bet with Léandre. Everything between us is a lie. *Everything.*"

Damien's nostrils flared. "And what are you hiding, Amelia? What is so important that you need to use us to get to the queen?"

His words were steady, offered with little inflection, as if he was holding back, but they pierced my heart like a shard of glass. Especially the use of my real name. I reached for the note as the tears began to fall. "Because," I said, thrusting it at him, "she's my sister."

I turned and ran from the ballroom. From Damien.

I hoped to never see him again.

Damien

I stared at Miel's retreating back, shock waving over me, the folded paper she'd given me still warm from her skin. My legs seemed rooted to the spot.

Sister, she'd said. But Kami didn't have a sister. Yet Miel did look like Kami—not her coloring, but the structure of her face, the blues of her eyes, and even the build of her body, though Kami was taller.

Harper and Emerson rushed up to us. "Where's Mel?" Harper asked, practically shouting in my face. "What did you do?"

"Me? Nothing."

"Well, you *were* acting a bit odd," Léandre said. "Why didn't you tell Amelia you're a count? Or introduce her to Kami? It's not as if she was going to hit Kami up for money or something."

I rounded on him. "You're the one who thought she'd be after my money. You set up that ridiculous wager!"

Léandre snorted. "I didn't expect you to keep going after you got that first date. It's not as if she's a pauper. Five million dollars may not be big in our circles, but it's not shabby."

"Five million?" I said at the same time Harper said, "You're a count?"

"This is crazy." Emerson turned on his heel. "I'm going to find Mel."

I wanted to grab him and keep him away from her, but the memory of the hurt in Miel's eyes made me let him go. Even if he was the one who comforted her, and not me, I wanted her to have someone.

"Text me when you do," Harper called after him before turning back to me. "So why on earth would Mel care about your money or title?"

"Oh, it happens all the time," Léandre said, and Bridgit nodded in agreement.

"Not with Mel, it doesn't. Even if she didn't have money, none of that would matter. But for the record, after her grandmother died, she was set up for life. Just because she doesn't flaunt it like the rest of you snobs doesn't mean she's poor."

"I had no idea," I said.

Harper shrugged. "Of course not. Emerson and I told her not to tell you. You might have chased her for it."

Frustration filled me. "I don't need her money!"

"Calm down." Léandre laid a hand on my shoulder. "They didn't know that."

"And how did *you* find out about Miel's finances?" I retorted.

"I did a background check on her, of course," said Léandre. "And when the report came back, I wanted to let you know I approved. Why else do you think I showed up at your place?" He raised a brow at my grimace. "Hey, what's the problem? I thought you'd have her checked out too."

"No, I didn't have her checked out! Everything was perfect

until tonight when she—" I broke off, remembering the note, now half crumpled in my hand. I looked at Harper. "She said something about Kami being her sister?"

Harper was folding her arms, glaring at me. "That's right. She found a letter from her birth father, and he talked about his other daughter. Of course, at the time Mel had no idea Kami had married your king. After she finally tracked Kami down, Mel booked this trip and begged us to come along. She wanted to meet her sister." Harper hesitated a few moments before adding, "She decided to see what kind of a person Kami was first, and I think she was right to be hesitant." Angry tears started in Harper's eyes. "It wouldn't be the first time Mel's been hurt."

And I'd hurt her again. "What should I do?"

"I think you've done enough." With that, Harper turned her back on me and strode purposefully away.

I stood there feeling empty. I'd blown it by not telling Miel the truth sooner. Maybe then she would have told me about Kami, and I could have arranged a better meeting. I could have prevented everything that went wrong tonight.

This was my fault.

"Well?" Léandre said. "Are you just going to stand there? Go after her, man."

His command shook me out of my misery. "Right. Okay, but I need you to do something for me." I opened the letter and scanned it quickly. Yes, this would be enough. Giving him the letter, I explained what I wanted. Then without another word, I ran toward the door.

I searched the parking lot, talked to waiting drivers, and combed the accessible parts of the palace, all the while calling and texting Miel. Nothing. She wasn't picking up, at least not my calls. Despair filled me.

I had to find her.

Chapter 13

Amelia

I'd left my shawl and purse back at the palace, and I didn't know exactly how I'd get home without money, but I was going to try. Even if I had to hitchhike or walk for three days. I removed my heels and made my way gingerly over the cobblestones. They no longer held the heat from the day, and I was already cold. The streets were very narrow, and everything looked so different from California. I wish I at least had my phone to text Emerson and Harper.

A tear skidded down my cheek. Not yet. I had to hold it together.

Footsteps behind me sent shivers of fear curling through my body. It was late, and I had no idea where I was except somewhere in the maze of streets outside the palace grounds. I turned, holding my heels in my hand as a potential weapon.

"Miel!" the figure called.

Damien. My heart that had seemed barely able to beat two

seconds ago jump-started back to life. I turned around and kept walking. He caught up to me.

"Go away."

"No," he said. "I'm not going away. Not now or ever."

I stopped and stared at him. "What do you want? I'm not after your money. I don't care about your stupid title. I just wanted—" *You,* I finished silently. "You know what? I have nothing to say to you." My heart pounded furiously at the lie; it was saying everything, but I hoped he couldn't hear it.

Damien touched me tentatively on the arm, but I pulled away. "I'm sorry, Miel. I should have told you the truth about myself. I'd planned to last night, but then you asked about the ball and I—"

"Thought I had ulterior motives!"

He nodded. "Even if you did, I should have made you tell me why the ball was so important to you—I knew that it was. But I didn't know about your inheritance then, and things have happened before in my life that made me worry . . ." He shook his head. "I still should have known. I should have wondered more why you'd take a job at the lodge when you have an engineering degree." He let that hang for a moment, his face etched with earnestness. "I'm so sorry I wasn't someone you could trust with your secret."

He was right. I hadn't trusted him. And why not? I'd been willing to tell Léandre but not him.

Because he means too much. I didn't want to scare him away.

But Harper had been right about us both hiding things, and maybe his fears had been as great as my own. It wasn't every day you met someone who stole your breath and made your knees weak.

"The thing is," Damien continued, taking my hand that wasn't holding the shoes, and this time I didn't pull away, "I think I'm falling in love with you. When I close my eyes . . . I can't imagine a future without you. And right now, I'm standing here dying inside because I'm so afraid that I've blown it. That you won't give us another chance. I'd like to make it up to you. Please?"

I blinked and two more tears splashed down my cheeks. Taking a deep breath, I said, "I don't know if I should. After all, now that you know about my inheritance, you're probably just after my money."

He gaped at me, and it was all I could do to keep a straight face. Then one edge of his mouth twitched upward, and we started laughing—or cry-laughing, because it wasn't exactly normal. I let him pull me to his chest. He felt warm and familiar, and I wanted to stay there forever.

"Now I'm sure of it," he whispered in my ear. "I really do love you."

I wanted to say it too, because one moment my world had seemed like it was over, and now I was alive again. If that wasn't love, what was?

But I couldn't say it just yet. That moment when I'd left the ballroom, too many of my emotions mirrored those I'd felt the night Jud had left me on the porch of my grandmother's house. Damien wasn't that man—I knew that—and I believed him, but I needed time.

I held him more closely. "I want to know it all. Tell me everything."

"Okay, but first there's somewhere I need to take you."

*D*amien led me back to the palace, by a route I would have never been able to find, and once there, we went through a corridor that was being guarded to prevent the public from entering. The two guards nodded and let him pass.

"Where are we going, Damien?"

His hand held mine that much tighter "Just a moment more. Trust me."

We wound through several hallways, each more elegant than the last. Finally, he stepped to an open doorway, and when I held back, he gave my hand a little tug. Slowly, I allowed him to draw me into the room, catching my breath when I saw who was inside.

Kami stood there with her husband, Gabriel Lacort, King of Beaumont. Léandre and Stéphanie were also nearby, as well as Harper and Emerson. Kami took one look at me and opened her arms. I hesitated, but Damien pushed me gently toward her.

"Oh, Amelia," Kami whispered through her tears, "I remember that doll. Daddy and I went shopping for it the first day they let him out of prison. He said it was for a little blond girl that I would meet soon, one who was going to be my best friend. I thought it was his way of being sneaky about picking out a decent Christmas present for me, even though I was almost too old for dolls and never played with them. It didn't matter, as long as he'd finally be around, you know?"

I did only too well.

"Then he died, and I forgot about it. Until tonight." She hugged me. "I'm so glad you came. So very, very glad Daddy was actually telling the truth. We will be best friends, just like he promised."

I hugged her back, letting the tears I'd been holding back for so long fall as I clung to her, this stranger, my older sister, who was happy to see me.

I knew in that moment everything was going to be all right.

Thank you, I mouthed to Damien.

He smiled and mouthed back, *I love you.*

or the next few months, the media was full of stories about Kami being reunited with her long-lost sister. Five more sisters and three brothers suddenly popped out of the woodwork, but they were quickly proven to be imposters. Kami and I even laughed about it on national TV. She disliked all the attention as much as I did, but she'd also had a difficult life growing up, and we used the publicity to bring in funds to help other abandoned or neglected children.

I never returned to work at the lodge—and thankfully they were more than content with the added news coverage they received because of my short tenure there. After my friends and I spent a few weeks at the palace to get to know Kami, we went to Damien's estate, where his mother and the servants smothered me with food and love.

Every moment that he wasn't working, Damien and I spent together, either alone or with our friends. I didn't think about the time passing or what awaited me in America. Damien's mother and sister had become so close to me that leaving them would be almost as hard as leaving Damien and Kami. For the first time since my mother died, I was part of a family.

Today we were out riding horses again. "Wait, I recognize this area," I said to Damien when I saw the bluff he'd brought me to that first day. Now I knew it didn't just overlook any beautiful valley, but his land, his enormous manor, his olive tree groves, and his factory, one of four that he owned.

He laughed and jumped off his horse, reaching for me. I slid into his arms, where he kissed me briefly before setting me on my feet. I had my own boots now, a custom-made gift from my sister, and Damien teased that I'd wear them to bed if I could. I didn't confess that I'd been tempted the first week after she'd given them to me.

Leaving the horses to graze, we walked hand in hand around the trees to the edge of the bluff. Thoughts of the future that I'd been studiously ignoring hit me hard, and it suddenly was difficult to swallow past the huge lump in my throat. In two weeks I was supposed to fly home. Kami and Gabriel had already offered me a challenging job here working with the royal civil engineers, and I wanted to take the job to be near Damien, but we hadn't discussed it yet. I sensed he was giving me time, waiting for when I could say I loved him.

"This is where we had our first kiss," Damien said, still holding my hand. "Do you remember? It wasn't the first time I wanted to kiss you, though."

I nodded. "I about kicked Emerson for not leaving us alone after we ate at Papa Amorosi's."

Damien laughed. "I wanted to kick him too. Hard." For long moments neither of us spoke. His eyes glittered in the sunlight— not like gold, but with a future full of promises.

He took a deep breath and pulled a ring from his pocket. Slipping it into my hand, he closed his fingers around mine and knelt on the rocky ground.

"I knew almost from the moment I first kissed you that you held my future in your hands. I love you, *Miel*, and I want you to stay here with me in Beaumont and share all this." He glanced briefly out over the valley. "I want to bring our children here and show them their land. I want to build a new tree house and wrestle with them in the mud field. Please, will you do me the honor of becoming my wife?"

"Yes." The words were out of my mouth before I could think twice about them. "I'd love to marry you."

He hesitated a second, then rose and kissed me with a long

lingering touch that would have banished any doubts—if I'd had any.

I didn't. That heavy lump of gold and jewels in my palm, probably a family heirloom, meant nothing next to the promise in his eyes. With a deep breath, I said the words he was waiting for: "I love you, Damien."

"Ah, finally!" he said with an exaggerated sigh. "I was beginning to think you were only after my money." He laughed and kissed me again.

*R*achel Branton has worked in publishing for over twenty years. She loves writing women's fiction and traveling, and she hopes to write and travel a lot more. As a mother of seven, it's not easy to find time to write, but the semi-ordered chaos gives her a constant source of writing material. She's been known to wear pajamas all day when working on a deadline, and is often distracted enough to burn dinner. (Okay, pretty much 90% of the time.) Under the name Rachel Branton, she writes romance, romantic suspense, and women's fiction. Rachel also writes urban fantasy, paranormal romance, and science fiction under the name Teyla Branton. For more information or to sign up to hear about new releases, please visit www.RachelBranton.com.

Note from the author: Thank you for spending a little time with me in my world. I hope you'll also check out my other books, beginning with *House Without Lies (Lily's House Book 1)* that tells the stories of more girls who grew up like Amelia and Kami. You can find a list of all my novels at the beginning of this book. Thanks again!